PUFFIN BOOKS

Andrew Cope lives slap bang in the middle of England, near a wonderful place called Derby. He supports his local footy team, even though they're rubbish. Three years ago he visited the RSPCA and adopted a cute puppy called Lara. She looks a bit like the dog on the cover and she really does have one sticky-up ear. Andrew suspects she might be a highly trained super spy who has gone undercover as a family pet. He thinks she could be the world's most top secret spy, which explains why he's never actually seen her on a mission.

Books by Andrew Cope

Spy Dog
Spy Dog 2
Spy Dog Unleashed!

SPY DOG
UNLEASHED!

ANDREW COPE

Illustrated by Chris Mould

PUFFIN

PUFFIN BOOKS

Published by the Penguin Group
Penguin Books Ltd, 80 Strand, London WC2R 0RL, England
Penguin Group (USA) Inc., 375 Hudson Street, New York, New York 10014, USA
Penguin Group (Canada), 90 Eglinton Avenue East, Suite 700, Toronto, Ontario, Canada M4P 2Y3
(a division of Pearson Penguin Canada Inc.)
Penguin Ireland, 25 St Stephen's Green, Dublin 2, Ireland (a division of Penguin Books Ltd)
Penguin Group (Australia), 250 Camberwell Road, Camberwell, Victoria 3124, Australia
(a division of Pearson Australia Group Pty Ltd)
Penguin Books India Pvt Ltd, 11 Community Centre, Panchsheel Park, New Delhi – 110 017, India
Penguin Group (NZ), 67 Apollo Drive, Rosedale, North Shore 0632, New Zealand
(a division of Pearson New Zealand Ltd)
Penguin Books (South Africa) (Pty) Ltd, 24 Sturdee Avenue, Rosebank, Johannesburg 2196, South Africa

Penguin Books Ltd, Registered Offices: 80 Strand, London WC2R 0RL, England

puffinbooks.com

Published 2007
This edition produced for The Book People Ltd,
Hall Wood Avenue, Haydock, St Helens, WA11 9UL

1

Set in Bembo
Typeset by Palimpsest Book Production Limited, Grangemouth, Stirlingshire
Made and printed in England by Clays Ltd, St Ives plc

British Library Cataloguing in Publication Data
A CIP catalogue record for this book is available from the British Library

ISBN: 978-0-141-33674-9

www.greenpenguin.co.uk

Mixed Sources
Product group from well-managed
forests and other controlled sources
www.fsc.org Cert no. SA-COC-1592
© 1996 Forest Stewardship Council

Penguin Books is committed to a sustainable future
for our business, our readers and our planet.
The book in your hands is made from paper
certified by the Forest Stewardship Council.

For Gonny and Great-grandad

Thanks to:

Mark
What can I say? A chance meeting at the school gates. I ran home to add the finishing touches. Cheers, mate.

Sarah and the team at Puffin
Sarah for being brilliant and the rest of the team for making it happen. I still can't believe it!

Chris
Long-overdue thanks. The illustrations always make me grin.

Lou
As always, for help, support and encouragement.

Staff and pupils at the following schools:
Curzon Primary, Quarndon
Holy Trinity Primary, Burton
Melbourne Junior, Derbyshire
Melbourne Infant, Derbyshire
Packington, near Ashby
Dame Catherine Harpur, Ticknall
Woodville, near Swadlincote
Orchard Primary, Castle Donington
Year 7s at Chellaston, Derby

Contents

1. A Well-earned Break

Mr Peacock was thoroughly enjoying his holiday. It was great to be away from the stress of work. He was still struggling to switch off but was enjoying getting up early, sitting on his balcony and watching the sun rise.

He poured himself a coffee and took in a lungful of crisp dawn air. He could see an early-morning waterskier skimming across the lake. He smiled. 'Someone else who can't sleep.'

Even at this distance he could tell the waterskier was excellent. First they expertly twisted and turned, pulling out wide and accelerating through the churning water. Then he watched in awe as the speedboat reached top speed and the skier shot up a ramp, somersaulted in the air and landed perfectly on the water.

Mr Peacock nodded in admiration as he sipped his coffee. 'I wish I could do that,' he sighed. The boat was now speeding towards him. He focused on the skier, who seemed to be waving to someone on the shore.

Mr Peacock rubbed his eyes. 'It can't be,' he muttered. He stood up and gripped the balcony rail, squinting into the distance. 'It can't be, but it is!'

He reached for his binoculars and fixed them to his eyes. The skier was now in focus and there was no doubt. He lowered the binoculars and took a deep breath before fixing them to his eyes once more. He could clearly see a waterskiing dog! It was weaving back and forth behind the speedboat, then up the next ramp, high

into the air . . . and smack on to the water. He watched the dog wobble a bit before it waved once more to its friend. He was sure the mutt was smiling! He watched as the canine skier blew imaginary kisses to the boat skipper.

Mr Peacock's heartbeat had risen and he was beginning to feel the same stress as at work. 'A waterskiing dog? Am I going mad?'

He strode into his apartment and shook his wife awake.

'Margaret,' he hissed. 'You've got to get up. There's something strange that I want you to see.'

His wife stirred slowly. Her eyelids opened a fraction.

'Clive,' she croaked, glancing at the clock, 'it's four thirty in the morning. Just because you can't sleep doesn't mean you have to wake me.'

'But, Margaret, there's something important, outside. Come quickly.'

His wife reluctantly pulled on her dressing gown and followed him out on to the balcony. She had rarely seen her husband so excited. He bounced up and down and pointed to the lake.

'Look, Margaret. Look over there at that waterskier and tell me what you see,' he gabbled.

His wife pulled her dressing gown tight against the cold morning air and frowned. She screwed up her eyes, squinting at the dot of a waterskier.

'Here, you'll need these,' Mr Peacock said, handing her the binoculars.

His wife put the binoculars to her sleepy eyes and scanned the lake, searching for the waterskier. She swept across the vast expanse of water until she found him, magnified greatly by the binoculars. Her eyes focused on the boy as he attempted a jump. She watched him land flat on his face and then float in his life jacket while the speedboat circled to pick him up.

'Excellent,' she murmured. 'But he does look like he needs a bit more practice.'

She watched as the skipper heaved the

boy back into the boat. There was a black-and-white dog in the boat and Mrs Peacock smiled as it licked the boy enthusiastically.

Her husband grabbed the binoculars. He watched the boy high-fiving the skipper. Mr Peacock lowered the binoculars.

'But . . .' he began, 'it wasn't the boy who was skiing. A minute ago it was the . . . the . . . thing,' he said, his voice trailing away.

'What *thing,* dearest?' asked his wife, a worried smile fixed on her lips.

'The thing . . . you know . . . the dog,' he said, knowing he sounded ridiculous. 'It really was.' His eye twitched like it always did when he was stressed.

Mrs Peacock was sympathetic. She knew how hard he'd been working before she had persuaded him to take a holiday and she knew that twitch.

'The dog was skiing? Of course it was, dearest,' she smiled. 'But we've come here for you to rest. I think you need to unwind and try and catch up on some sleep,' she soothed. Things were obviously worse than she'd imagined. She led him back inside and tucked him up under the duvet. She watched her husband lying there, his twitching eye working overtime.

He kept muttering to himself, 'A waterskiing dog . . .?'

In the boat, Ben and his dad high-fived again.

'Great effort, mate,' praised Dad. 'Not quite as good as Lara yet, but you're getting there.'

Lara wagged her tail proudly.

I agree, she thought, licking Ben affectionately. *A bit more practice and you'll be able to do those tricky jumps. It's a shame we have to ski so early, but it's the only time I'm allowed to practise. We don't want anyone knowing my secret identity. And there's little chance of anyone seeing us this early in the morning.*

The pet steered the speedboat back to shore where the rest of her family was waiting.

'Brilliant, Lara!' shouted Sophie as they approached the wooden jetty. 'You are one amazing pooch!'

I was pretty good, wasn't I? thought Lara,

wagging her tail vigorously as she climbed out of the speedboat.

'Hey, what about me?' said Sophie's older brother. 'I did pretty well too, don't you think?'

Sophie smiled politely. 'Getting there, Ben,' she agreed. 'I don't know about you skiers but I'm starving. Can we have breakfast now?'

Lara nodded and wagged enthusiastically. *There's nothing like a bit of early-morning waterskiing to work up an appetite. Mine's a full English,* she thought as the family wandered off to find a cafe. *With extra sausages. Don't you just love holidays?*

2. A Cunning Plan

Mr Big sat in his prison cell trying to act as if it was just another day. He couldn't help fidgeting with excitement. Tonight was the night he was going to escape. It was all set for midnight. He sat on his chair and threw a dart at the dartboard. And another, this time much harder. It hit the black-and-white dog in the picture right between the eyes, and he smiled.

At nine o'clock the guard did his last patrol and Mr Big heard the familiar clunk as the bolt on the door to his cell slid into place.

'Sweet dreams,' the guard smirked through the grille. 'Be a good boy and don't get up to any mischief. Be seeing you in the morning as usual.'

'You may be surprised,' murmured Mr Big as the lights went out. He lay and thought about how things had changed since he'd been in prison.

'It's all that dog's fault,' he told himself. 'It destroyed my wonderful life. Everything I worked so hard for is now gone. I've lost my homes, my yacht and my freedom. Spy Dog, they call her. Dead Dog, more like.'

The master criminal lay on his hard mattress and looked at the luminous dial on his wristwatch. Two hours, fifty-eight minutes and eighteen . . . seventeen . . . sixteen seconds to go. Once he was on the outside he would find that dog. Mr Big lay wide-eyed, watching the seconds ticking away and planning his revenge.

3. A Perfect Catch

The Cook family was having a fabulous time. Mum had insisted on a proper holiday where nothing could go wrong. Since they had adopted Lara from the RSPCA, the children had got involved in all sorts of adventures so Mum was delighted that, for once, this holiday was going according to plan. Ben had persuaded her that it would be OK to go to the Lake District.

'It's the most boring place in the world, Mum,' he'd said. 'I mean, what trouble could we possibly get into?'

Mum and Dad were now aware of Lara's secret identity. Their adopted family pooch had turned out to be a highly trained Spy Dog, the government's first-ever Licensed Assault and Rescue Animal. In fact, they hadn't adopted Lara at all – she had chosen them as part of her escape plan from the RSPCA. Her Secret Service owners called her by her code name, GM451, but the family preferred to call her Lara – it was cute and it suited her.

Mum and Dad relaxed while they watched Lara playing with Ben, Sophie and their little brother Ollie. Lara was joining in with a game of cricket, fielding at silly point. She was now firmly part of the family and they all loved having her around. Everyone was very careful to keep Lara's special abilities secret. The children knew that if her identity were ever revealed she would have to leave them, so activities like water-skiing were arranged for early morning, when most people were asleep.

Their game of cricket was played well away from the main group of holidaymakers. Lara was an excellent fielder. Like all dogs, she could catch with her mouth. However, she'd recently discovered that by wearing a baseball mitt she could also catch with her paws and she soon had Sophie out, taking a spectacular diving catch in her left glove.

How's that? she howled as she threw the

ball into the air in delight. *Another result for the marvellous mutt.*

Mum and Dad watched as Lara took her turn at batting. The dog gripped the bat firmly in her mouth and went through a couple of practice strokes.

I've seen cricket on the telly, she thought. *I'm sure it can't be too difficult.*

Ben waited patiently as his dog went through another couple of practice strokes like she'd seen the England cricketers do.

OK, ready, Lara indicated to Ben the bowler.

He glanced around to check nobody was watching. There was a couple walking along the path but they were a long way off, so he galloped up to the wicket and released an excellent ball which zinged towards Lara at alarming speed.

Yikes, a fast one! No wonder they wear helmets.

The family pet had very little time to react. She instinctively swung the bat and belted the ball back over Ben's head.

Looks like a six. Lara held her breath. She had hit the ball too well.

The family watched in open-mouthed silence as the tennis ball arced through the air towards the couple on the path. At the last moment the man saw the ball coming. He dropped his ice cream and caught the ball. His eye twitched as he looked up and saw the dog, bat in mouth, guilty look on its face.

Woops! Sorry about your ice cream.

It was the same dog he'd seen waterskiing earlier that day. Now it was playing cricket!

'Margaret,' Mr Peacock began, 'did you see that?'

'Yes, a terrific catch, dearest,' she smiled. 'Very well done.'

'No, did you see who hit the ball, Margaret?' he said pointing to the beach.

Lara had quickly dropped the bat and Sophie was now standing at the wicket. Lara was digging a hole in the sand, like she thought normal dogs did.

Just be normal, dig, dig, dig, she thought.

Mrs Peacock looked down at the beach and saw the bat in Sophie's hand. 'Great shot, young lady,' she shouted, throwing the ball back to the players.

'But it wasn't the girl, Margaret,' insisted her husband. 'It was the . . . the . . . thing like last time.'

He pointed frantically to the digging dog. His wife linked arms and guided her husband back towards the hotel.

'The dog hit a six,' he explained.

'Of course it did, dearest,' soothed his wife. 'Dogs do that, don't they.'

Mrs Peacock was determined to make her husband take things easy for the rest of the week.

4. The Great Escape

The seconds ticked away until all three of the luminous hands on Mr Big's watch pointed to midnight. He rose from his bed and tucked his pillow under the blanket so it looked like a sleeping prisoner. He shivered as he strode over to the portrait of the queen hanging on his cell wall. Quickly but silently he took a screwdriver from its hiding place and removed the portrait. The hole in the wall was even darker than his cell. He squeezed through the blackness and felt his way down the hand-made steps before jumping into a wider opening – his 'tunnel of revenge'. He found the water pipe and tapped on it three times with the screwdriver. He waited impatiently.

'Come on, come on,' he whispered.

He heard three taps echoing back up the pipe and knew the coast was clear. Mr Big crawled through the darkness and into the next air vent, before dropping into the prison officers' changing room.

'This is so easy,' he whispered, spitting dirt out of his mouth and dusting himself down.

He struggled out of his filthy prisoner's clothes and into the neatly folded officer's uniform that had been conveniently left for him. At that moment the door opened and in strolled two men, dressed smartly in similar officer's uniforms. Mr Big broke into a huge smile.

'Good to see you, boys,' he said, slapping them both on the back. 'And don't you look fabulous in your new clothes.'

'Thanks, boss,' grinned the first prisoner, who was as big as an ape. 'Are you sure this is gonna work?' he asked nervously.

'You're out of your cells, aren't you?' smiled Mr Big. 'Trust me. Soon the three of us will be on the other side, free as birds. Follow me. And, whatever you do, don't look worried.'

The three prisoners walked down the corridor: Mr Big striding confidently and his accomplices following gingerly. The ape-like man was lolloping along, his body almost splitting his uniform. The smaller man scampered beside him, tripping over his trousers, which were too long for his short legs. They heard voices up ahead and Mr Big swung the trio into a laundry room. It was humid and the drone of the washers and dryers made it difficult to hear as some real prison officers went by. Mr Big put his ear to the door, listening hard.

All three prisoners jumped as a voice piped up from behind them, 'Yes, officers, what can I do for you?'

The three criminals turned to look. It was Dave 'Dirt Bag' Smith, a fellow prisoner assigned to work in the laundry room. Dirt Bag looked at the uniforms and then at the faces. Something wasn't quite right. He twigged almost immediately.

'M–Mr B–Big,' he spluttered, saucer-eyed. 'And Archie. And Gus. What are you guys doing dressed as prison officers?'

No answer was required. Dirt Bag's eyes

opened even wider as he realized they were about to escape. His mind whirred into action. He was serving a life sentence and wanted to escape too.

'Guys,' he pleaded, 'take me with you. I want out.' He looked at their blank faces. 'I'm beggin' you, please.'

Mr Big mulled it over for less than a second. His plan involved only three people. They had only three uniforms. He couldn't risk it.

'Sorry, Dirt Bag,' he growled. 'No can do.'

'I'll raise the alarm,' said Dirt Bag defiantly. He knew not to mess with Mr Big, but he was desperate. A life sentence sure was a long time. 'If I can't go over the wall, neither can you,' he gambled.

Mr Big looked at his watch. He had no more time to waste. If he was to escape tonight, as planned, he needed to move now.

'Then I have no choice,' he said menacingly. 'Boys, please clean the Dirt Bag.'

Gus smiled, his gold teeth glinting, as he grabbed Dirt Bag Dave and expertly hauled him over to a washing machine.

'No. Please, no,' begged Dirt Bag. 'I was only joking. I'd never grass you up, really. Have mercy.'

Mr Big looked puzzled. He didn't do mercy and, besides, he couldn't take the chance. He nodded at his two helpers. 'Do it.'

Dirt Bag went into the machine. It was a big machine but it was still a tight squeeze and he put up a fight. Finally his kicking legs were stuffed in and the door slammed. Mr Big and his helpers looked at Dirt Bag, scrunched up inside the washing machine. He looked very uncomfortable. They could see his face and a foot jammed against the round window. His pleading cries were muffled.

'What now?' asked the smaller man. 'Do we just leave him here?'

Mr Big shrugged. 'By the time they find him we'll be long gone,' he smiled.

He took a moment to study his map before the three fake officers

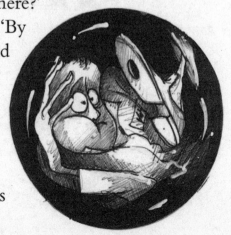

straightened their uniforms and boldly strolled out of the laundry room, through the officers' quarters, and into the prison car park.

It was pouring with rain. Mr Big spotted the prison van.

'That's the one,' he shouted over the din of the storm. 'It should be open with the keys in.'

The three escapees sprinted across the car park and jumped in. Mr Big's heart was pounding as he started the engine and headed towards the security barrier. The

wipers were struggling to cope, even at double speed. He patted the revolver in his jacket pocket. If the barrier wouldn't open then he may need to use force. It was nearly 1 a.m. and the man on the gate was half asleep. Mr Big pulled up at the barrier, lowered his window and waved his fake identity card. His body stiffened for a moment as a torch shone in his face. But the barrier rose and Mr Big saluted. He crunched the van into gear and accelerated out into the free world.

The three escapees waited until they were well away from the prison walls before they celebrated. The van trundled through the storm as Gus and Archie leaped around in the back, hugging, back-slapping and grinning from ear to ear.

'No more prison food,' sang Gus.

'No more lights out at nine,' trumpeted Archie.

'And no more digging the tunnel of revenge,' growled Mr Big, looking at the dirt under his fingernails.

After the celebrations died down Mr Big put on his serious voice.

'OK, we're out,' he announced. 'That's the easy bit. Now the real work begins. We are about to pull off the biggest crime in history, but what do we do first?'

The two thugs knew the plan inside out. Mr Big puffed his chest with pride as they chorused, 'First, we get rid of the dog.'

5. Ready, Steady, Cook

Ben was the eldest of the three children. He and Lara had become the best of friends and they spent hours together playing outside. The pair often camped in the back garden or went for long bike rides. They would take a picnic of Lara's favourite banana and salami sandwiches and spend lazy afternoons fishing by the river. Ben was handsome and always managed to be cool without really trying. His natural good humour meant he was popular at school, more so now that he had Lara.

Some of his school mates knew of Lara's special status, but had promised to keep her secret. They loved having their very own Spy Dog in the neighbourhood and were delighted when she was allowed into school.

Lara sometimes came in to demonstrate web design or to show the children how to do martial arts, but her favourite lesson was PE. Lara was especially good at football, hockey and gymnastics.

Lara liked to think of herself as unusual-looking, although her keen ears had picked up remarks on her ugliness from one or two passers-by. This never upset her because she knew that beauty was only skin deep.

I may be unusual on the outside, she decided, *but I am very special on the inside*.

She was a medium-sized dog, mostly white with black splodges over her body. Her markings were similar to those of a Friesian cow. She had black-and-white whiskers and a tail that wagged around like helicopter blades. When she met the children off the school bus she sometimes felt like she'd take off with the excitement. Her tongue was extra-long, especially after a cross-country fitness run or her morning press-ups. She knew that her ears were a bit odd, especially the one that permanently stood to attention. Recently she'd spent long hours in front of the mirror trying to stiffen her floppy one. But no amount of ear-obics would get it to stand upright. It didn't matter what she looked like, the Cook family loved her.

Lara was glad to have left the Secret Service.

Sure, they spent millions on training me in the latest spying techniques and their intensive teaching programme has made me the most intelligent animal on the planet, but family life is much better than the life of a secret agent. And this holiday is fantastic, she thought, turning the sausages on the barbecue. *How many families would trust their mutt to cook?* she asked herself, adjusting her chef's hat. The only things she really missed about being a spy were the gadgets. She'd had all sorts of fun with electric collars, alphabet dog biscuits and the lab's special chemical formulas.

No need for those any more though, she thought, sipping her milkshake through a straw.

Mr Peacock sauntered down the road, twitching ever so slightly. It was close to his teatime and the smell of sausages cooking on a barbecue was making him drool. He could see smoke rising from behind the hedge and wondered what his wife would be making for his tea. Lara had been careful to set the barbecue up in a quiet spot, almost hidden from passers-by. She hadn't realized the hedge had a low point that nosy neighbours could see over. Mr Peacock couldn't help but look. He could see the top of a chef's hat. As he walked on and the hedge dipped he could gradually see more of the hat – and the wearer. He spied an ear, a furry one with a hole in. His eye was twitching alarmingly now as he stopped

in his tracks and shook his head. This walk was meant to clear his head of waterskiing, cricketing dogs and now here was a pooch chef. He gawped over the hedge and saw Lara cooking sausages and burgers on the barbie. He twitched in amazement as the mutt sauntered over to a deckchair and picked up a book. She fixed her glasses on the end of her nose and settled into a good read, noisily sipping the last of her milkshake.

Ahh, perfect, she thought. *Shaken not stirred. Just the way I like it.*

Mr Peacock quickened his pace in an effort to catch up with his wife.

'Margaret,' he shouted, 'I think I need to see a doctor.'

As they sat down to eat, the Cook family marvelled at Lara's skill. She was delighted that her first-ever barbecue had been such a success. Lara looked at her family's happy faces and thought about her old life as a Spy Dog. *It was certainly more exciting but this is where I really belong.*

Lara cringed at the memory of one dangerous mission that had gone terribly wrong. She had been shot by a horrible criminal, Mr Big, who was now safely behind bars.

He's got twenty-five years to think about the error of his ways, she sighed. It gave her great satisfaction to know that she'd put an end to his drug-smuggling business. *He's lost all his ill-gotten gains.* She smiled as she remembered catching him.

She'd had to bite his bottom and wait for the police to arrive. She knew he was a very clever man. He had already escaped the police once and, before Lara caught him, he'd shot her several times. She put her paw to her ear and felt one of the bullet holes.

Boy, that had been close. But now, she thought, *the biggest risk I take is going waterskiing or perhaps letting the sausages spit at me on the barbie.*

Lara watched the kids munching on their burgers. She knew all three loved her but it was Ben who played with her the most. Sophie was very giggly – it was easy to make her laugh. All Lara had to do was pull a funny face or dance and Sophie would start to chuckle. She always had her head in a book and would spend hours writing stories or drawing pictures.

Ollie was the youngest but he had the most vivid imagination. He liked anything gruesome and could recall horrible stories about pirates and ogres, as if he'd actually been there. Lara loved messing about on his PlayStation and he was now only just about able to beat her. Little did Ollie know that while he was at nursery school she would spend most of the day practising her gaming skills. She had a very competitive streak.

Mum squirted some tomato sauce on to Lara's sausage.

Mmm, delicious. I've never tried one of these before, she thought after biting into it.

Dad waited until Lara had finished her first sausage before explaining that she'd just eaten a hot dog. Ben cracked up laughing at Lara's astonished face.

'Don't look so worried, Lara,' he laughed. 'They're not real dogs – that's just what they're called.'

Thank goodness for that, coughed Lara, rubbing her tummy and still looking a bit concerned.

Lara's teacher, Professor Cortex, would have frowned at burgers and sausages. As the head of Spy School, he had always insisted on healthy food, often mixed with his home-made brain formula that boosted intelligence. She felt guilty and reached for the salad bowl.

A bit of green stuff will probably do me good, she thought, nibbling a token sliver of cucumber.

She was grateful to the professor and his team for everything they'd done. She had come through Spy Dog training head and shoulders above all the other animals and this had given her massive confidence.

But I have to put that behind me now, she thought. *Just act normal. No more adventures.*

She had been warned that any more scrapes could result in her being taken away from her beloved family. She watched Ben, Sophie and Ollie munching happily and made herself a promise: *There's no way I'm leaving these kids.*

6. Breaking News

Mr Big and his fellow escapees settled into his apartment in London. It was total luxury and had cost him a packet but neither Gus nor Archie dared ask where he'd got the money from. Their bickering was already irritating him.

'Boss, he won't let me watch CBBC,' complained Gus. 'And he keeps telling me I'm stupid.'

Mr Big snatched the remote and flicked on the news. 'If you two goons can't agree then we'll watch something I want to watch,' he bellowed.

It was perfect timing. Hush descended as they saw news of their escape being broadcast on the BBC. Mr Big shuddered as a photo of him appeared on the screen.

'Terrible,' he moaned. 'That picture is taken from such a bad angle.'

Photos of the other two came up next and they immediately went into panic mode.

'Now everyone's going to recognize us,' whimpered Archie.

Mr Big looked at the pair and raised an eyebrow in agreement. They stood out a mile.

Gus took up nearly the whole settee and looked very dangerous. His massive body was scary enough but when you added his

bald head, flat nose and tattoos he looked even more menacing. He had a snarling smile, made worse when he revealed his gold teeth. Mr Big considered that if you met Gus in a dark alley you would simply hand over your wallet without him even asking. Gus was a good old-fashioned sort of criminal – not very clever, but totally reliable.

Archie was a different type altogether. His scarlet face and tiny features were almost lost in a mass of hair. His eyes continually darted around the room like he was waiting to be attacked. His eyebrows were bushy and the thick hair covering his back was springing out of the top of his shirt. Mr Big was pleased to have Archie with him because what he lacked in strength he made up for in brains.

Mr Big signalled for hush and the unlikely trio focused once again on the news item. The reporter was standing outside the high-security prison under an umbrella. The heavy rain made it a difficult interview.

'And exactly how did they escape?' asked the presenter in the TV studio.

The reporter put his hand to his ear to listen harder. 'Well, it seems that they simply tunnelled out,' he shouted above the thundering rain. 'The gang seems to have been very well organized. They overpowered a fellow prisoner and, once out into the open, they broke into a van and drove through the gates.'

The reporter's umbrella blew inside out but, like the true professional he was, he carried on. 'The prison governor has been suspended and the Home Secretary has called for a full public enquiry because it's the first time anyone's ever escaped from this maximum-security prison.'

'And are the men dangerous?' asked the presenter.

'Extremely,' bawled the reporter. 'All three have long criminal records and the public are asked not to approach them.'

Mr Big flicked the TV off. He'd anticipated being on the news. It wasn't a problem. His criminal mind had been working on a cunning plan. Six months in prison had been time well spent.

'We're famous,' cheered Archie, bouncing on the settee. 'We're the first ones to ever escape from that prison.'

'And we're dangerous,' growled Gus, cracking his knuckles.

'Very dangerous indeed,' purred Mr Big. 'Especially if you're a black-and-white dog.'

The doorbell rang and Mr Big ordered Archie to check it out. He flicked on the CCTV monitor. The grainy picture showed a woman and a dog waiting outside. Mr Big nodded and Archie released the downstairs door. A minute later the woman knocked and Archie let her in. She and Mr Big embraced while the muzzled dog sat by her side.

'Here's what you asked for,' she said, pointing to the black-and-white dog. 'Meet Bambi. An exact replica of Spy Dog. Evil and vicious, as you ordered.'

The escapees stared at the dog. It looked a bit comical with one ear sticking up. The woman passed around a photo of Lara and the men marvelled at the likeness.

'Bambi's a stupid name for a dog,' said Archie. 'It's not very scary at all.'

'Bambi is a code name,' explained the woman. 'It stands for "Big Aggressive Menacing Bad Influence". And, believe you me, Bambi lives up to her name, hence the muzzle.'

Despite his size, Gus was a bit of a softy when it came to dogs.

'Hello, Bambi-Wambi,' he cooed, putting his hand out to stroke the animal.

Bambi issued a hands-off warning growl from behind her muzzle and Gus retreated, a worried look on his face.

'Excellent,' nodded Mr Big. 'And she looks exactly as I remember.' He rubbed his bottom where Lara had sunk her teeth in. 'How did you manage to get that ridiculous ear right?'

'Getting it to stand up required surgery,' explained the woman.

Mr Big nodded again. 'And have you trained Bambi as I asked?'

'Six months of intensive training,' answered the woman. 'You won't get a better animal. Follows instructions to the letter. She's supremely intelligent when she needs to be, but horrible with it. This dog is the canine equivalent of you – a calculating, evil, criminal genius.'

Mr Big loved compliments. He stroked his chin.

'Excellent,' he growled. 'I will leave you to complete the next part of the plan. Guys, you know what to do. I have an appointment with the best surgeon money can buy. See you in six weeks.'

Mr Big collected his bag and let himself out. The gang watched from the window as his Rolls swept out of the garage.

7. *Neighbourhood Watch*

The Cooks returned from their holiday and slipped back into their normal routine. Ben and Sophie went back to school, Ollie to nursery school and Mum and Dad went to work. Lara was home alone, but, as always, she tried to use her time wisely. Her latest mission was to organize the local pets into a neighbourhood-watch team. The assorted group of dogs and cats assembled on Tuesday and Thursday mornings to be put through their paces. George the tortoise always came too, usually setting off hours before, to get to the meetings on time. Lara wasn't quite sure how he'd ever come in useful, but she couldn't fault his positive attitude. The dogs and cats still eyed each other suspiciously. Lara had told them to put their differences aside for the sake of teamwork but Rex the Alsatian couldn't help licking his lips every time he looked at next door's tabby.

'You never know when we might need to catch a suspect,' Lara had told them at the last meeting.

They were all in awe of Lara, she was so clever. They wanted to work in the neighbourhood-watch team in the hope that some of her genius might rub off on them.

It was Tuesday morning and the pets were assembled in Lara's garden.

'OK,' she began. 'Remind me what we learned last time.'

Lara watched as the animals concentrated and tried to remember. Some weren't very clever. Rex couldn't get the tabby out of his mind. Jasper scratched at a flea and Ruby looked puzzled. Tiger couldn't remember what he'd had for breakfast that morning, never mind what they did last time.

Santa raised his paw as Lara had told them to. 'Er, last session we did search and rescue,' he recalled. 'You hid George and we sniffed him out.'

'Excellent, little fella,' barked Lara. Santa flushed with pride. 'Today's lesson is even more advanced. We are going to learn how to enter a house by an upstairs window. This technique can come in handy if there's a fire or maybe a burglar upstairs, maybe even if you're locked out one night. Who knows.'

The children's trampoline had been pushed up against the side of the house and Lara had dragged Mum's small keep-fit bouncer from the bedroom to go alongside it. Just before the meeting she had opened the upstairs bathroom window.

'Who's first?' She looked around at the volunteers. *Probably not George,* she considered.

'What have we got to do, Lara?' barked the Labrador from number six. 'Is it dangerous?'

'A bit,' admitted Lara. 'We learned this at Spy School so it's quite advanced.' She looked at the line of dogs and cats. 'Jimmy, what about you?' she asked. 'You're the bravest little Scottie I know. And you would easily fit through the window.'

Jimmy stood as tall as his stumpy legs would allow. He puffed his chest out with pride. *The bravest she knows, wow!* Like a soldier on parade, he stepped forward to volunteer his full pedigree name: 'James Highland Glen White Mist McDouglas at your service, ma'am.'

'OK,' smiled Lara. 'The run-up's even longer than your name. You leap on to the small bouncer, then on to the big one and finally through the upstairs window,' she barked, pointing upward. Jimmy looked less sure. 'Come on, Jimbo, I know you can do it. Give it a try.'

Jimmy nodded and ran off to the other end of the garden. He would need a good run-up just to get on to the trampoline. Lara gave him the nod and his scampering run-up began. George watched jealously as Jimmy's legs became a blur. He hurled himself on to the bouncer. *Weyhey!*

Then on to the trampoline. *Yeehah!*

He bounced up towards the window. *Wow, I'm flying*, he thought as he looked down at the open-mouthed team below. He managed a quick look over the trees to the river before he hit the house with a crunch. He slid down the wall and Lara caught him perfectly.

'Unlucky, Jimmy,' she soothed as she dusted him off. 'No permanent damage done. Plenty of spring, you just need a little practice with direction.' She looked around at the others who had all taken a step backward. 'Now, who's next . . .?'

8. A Menacing Mutt

The old lady couldn't believe that it had happened in broad daylight.

'So tell me once more, madam. It was definitely a black–and–white dog that robbed you?'

The lady was still shaking. 'Y–Yes, officer,' she stammered. 'I had just collected my pension and was walking home when the dog came up to me from the side. It knocked me off balance and snatched my handbag.'

'And then what, madam?' asked the policeman, licking his pencil like he'd seen police do in the movies.

'Well, I tried to grab it back but the dog growled at me. It stuck its nose in my bag and pulled out my purse, as if it knew exactly what it was looking for.' The lady composed herself a little. 'And then it ran off. I know it sounds absurd, officer, but I've been mugged by a mutt.'

'Mugged . . . by . . . a . . . mutt,' repeated the policeman as he scribbled on his notepad.

The policeman knocked on his boss's door.

'Another one, sarge,' he said sadly. 'This time an old dear, mugged in broad daylight. Same dog by the sounds of it.' He flipped open his notebook and read. 'Black-and-white splodges, medium size, one ear up and one ear down. "Mugged by a mutt". Just like the other descriptions.'

The sergeant beckoned him in. 'Sit down, PC Chandler,' he said. 'I've just been watching this.' He pointed to a flat-screen TV on the wall. 'It's the latest CCTV footage from the bank job last Monday.'

PC Chandler shook his head in disbelief as he

watched a black-and-white dog enter the High Street bank. The video footage switched to inside the bank and the policemen observed the dog waiting in the queue. One of the customers tried to stroke it and the dog snarled. A bank clerk came out and tried to shoo the animal away but it became angry and bared its teeth. The staff withdrew and the dog sat down.

'Watch what happens next,' said the sergeant as he fast-forwarded the video.

The men watched as customers sprinted in and out of the bank, the dog sitting patiently throughout. The sergeant took his finger off the fast-forward button and the video slowed. 'This is where it gets interesting,' he said.

The policemen watched as the security guard arrived to collect the day's takings and the dog attacked. It surprised the guard, grabbed the money bag in its teeth and made an easy getaway. The footage cut to the outside and the policemen watched as the dog bounded out of shot.

'That's the fourth one this week,' explained the sergeant, scratching his head. 'Bank, post

office, corner shop and now this mugging.'
He rewound the video to get a close-up of
the dog's face. The snarling animal was frozen
on screen, fangs on full view, its sticky-up
ear making it look faintly ridiculous.

'I want this dog caught,' he ordered. 'I
can't keep the press quiet much longer. If
we don't get to the bottom of this crime,
our force will be a laughing stock. I can
already see the "Canine Crime" headlines.'
The sergeant's fist banged on the table to
emphasize his words. 'All leave is cancelled.
I need every available officer patrolling the
streets and, just to be sure, I'm going to
contact higher authorities to enlist some
help.'

9. A Canine Crime Wave

Gus and Archie had enjoyed working with Bambi's trainer, Cynthia. She was a real expert in animal behaviour and the three followed Mr Big's orders precisely, even if some of his instructions were a bit unusual. It involved them moving out of his expensive London flat but this had been compensated for by the thrill of watching Bambi carry out some very clever crimes. They had spent six busy weeks in the Midlands. It had seemed strange that Mr Big had ordered each robbery to be done under the watchful gaze of a security camera.

They were especially proud of yesterday's crime, which had been the most difficult one yet. It had taken a great deal of preparation but it had been worth it.

Archie had checked the CCTV camera and given the thumbs-up. 'It's pointing right where we want it,' he'd said. 'Lights, camera . . . action!'

Bambi had wandered down the street, waiting for the right moment. As a bus had approached, she had walked out into the road. The driver had slammed his foot on the brake and the bus had jerked to a halt, throwing the passengers out of their seats. The driver leaped out of his cab and threw his hands to his head.

'Oh no,' he cried. 'Poor dog. She just ran out, honest. I couldn't do anything about it.'

Bambi lay still, waiting for the signal. Cynthia had blown her whistle and Bambi jumped up at the driver. Then the criminal dog had got on to the bus and started snarling viciously at the passengers. It was clear what she wanted. The CCTV camera had recorded the terrified passengers stuffing their watches, wallets and jewellery into a bag around the Bambi's neck. One teenager refused to hand over her iPod, earning a curled lip and snarl for her bravery. When the bag was full Bambi took off down the street, the courageous driver in hot pursuit. By the time he made it back to his passengers the police had arrived and were taking statements. PC Chandler had opened his notebook and licked his pencil.

'Don't tell me, sir,' he'd guessed, shaking his head, 'you've been hijacked by a black-and-white dog?'

It had been six weeks since Bambi had arrived and the gang had returned to Mr Big's expensive London flat. Wads of banknotes were piled up on the kitchen table. Stolen watches tumbled out of drawers and a fabulously expensive painting was newly installed above the fireplace. Bambi was indeed a perfect criminal. She had just the right mixture of skill, bravery and toughness.

Archie, Gus and Cynthia waited excitedly as Mr Big's Rolls-Royce swept into the garage, followed a few minutes later by the sound of a key in the door.

'Can't wait to show the boss what we've stolen,' grinned Archie, rubbing his hands in glee.

Their faces fell as a stranger entered the apartment. Bambi sniffed and growled, straining at her leash. Archie shot up from the sofa and started to sweep the piles of cash from view.

Gus lumbered towards the stranger. 'Oi, who are you? And what you doing in our pad?' he asked, gold teeth flashing beneath his curled lip.

'Sit down, guys,' ordered the stranger. 'And listen to the rest of the plan.' Gus was puzzled. He recognized the voice but not the face. 'And it's not your pad, it's mine.'

It took a moment to register.

'Boss?' asked Gus. 'Is it you . . .?'

'Of course it is, idiot,' came Mr Big's reply. 'I'm delighted you didn't recognize me. That means my surgery has been worthwhile. What do you think?'

Mr Big stood tall, sweeping his hands down his body, allowing the gang to admire his new look. They stared open-mouthed. He was slimmer for a start. The beer belly had disappeared. His new head of hair was blond and combed back. His face was almost unrecognizable. The squashed nose was now a cute ski slope. His flabby double chin had been replaced by a single, firm one and his cheeks lifted, film-star style. The dark 'suitcases' under his eyes were now just hand luggage and his teeth sparkled. Everything was a bit overdone and his face seemed a bit tight. But the surgeon had earned his money. Mr Big looked ten years younger, even if he did find it difficult to smile.

Cynthia sniffed. 'And that's a very powerful smell,' she said politely, almost overcome by the aftershave.

'Ah, yes,' Mr Big agreed. 'Sorry about that but I plan to meet that dratted Spy Dog. As you know, dogs have a good sense of smell, so I have had to change everything, including my aftershave. There's absolutely no way that Spy Dog will recognize me now.' Mr Big broke into as wide a smile as was possible with his new face. 'And guys, I'm no longer Mr Big, the criminal mastermind. Everything about me has changed.' The gang's boss took a deep breath and adjusted his voice into something much posher. 'I am now Sir Humphrey Goldfinger,' he announced in perfect Queen's English.

'Self-made billionaire, charity worker and, to the general public, all-round good guy. And this, my friends, is our latest criminal target,' he purred, walloping a rolled-up newspaper on to the table.

Archie pounced on it excitedly. ' "Millennium Diamond Exhibition opens on Saturday",' he read out loud. ' "The world's largest diamond will be on display at London's Natural History Museum. The gem, considered priceless, is normally kept under lock and key with the Crown jewels." '

He jumped off the sofa to avoid Gus who was trying to snatch the newspaper to read it for himself.

' "In a very rare public appearance, the diamond is going on general display." ' Archie paused to look at the others. Their thrilled faces mirrored his. His voice rose in excitement as he read the next sentence. ' "The exhibition is to be opened by multi-millionaire Sir Humphrey Goldfinger, who is kindly sponsoring the event." '

They all looked at Mr Big, whose glow was almost royal. Gus pointed at his boss and mouthed the words 'That's you'.

Archie continued,' "The diamond will be under close guard throughout its time in the museum and Sir Humphrey has pledged to make sure everything is done to ensure its safe-keeping." ' Archie punched the air in triumph while Gus started punching the wall, already practising knocking the guards out.

Mr Big's smile was now so big that he could feel his new face stretching tight under the strain. He lit a huge cigar and imagined what it would be like to be the richest man in the world. 'The Millennium Diamond will, of course, be perfectly safe,' he announced in his posh Sir Humphrey accent. 'Safely in my possession,' he roared. He looked at Cynthia. 'There is a little matter of a Spy Dog to attend to before we do the diamond theft.' He puffed on his massive cigar and disappeared in a cloud of grey smoke. 'If you've done your job properly, that horrible dog may already be behind bars.'

10. Dognapped

Every dog warden in the area had been called to a meeting. A large photograph of the snarling black-and-white dog had been beamed on to a big screen and the wardens offered a massive reward for the one who could catch it.

'It's a very dangerous animal,' explained the chief warden. 'It seems to have been on our patch for the last six weeks. Don't take any risks. We don't want to alarm the public. We must simply catch the mutt and deal with it.'

The dog catchers scurried off, eager to be the first to claim the reward.

Lara's Tuesday-morning neighbourhood-watch meeting had just broken up. Jimmy the Scottie had finally made it through the upstairs window. There had been a loud crash as he hit the bathroom mirror so Lara had gone up to check that he hadn't bashed his nose too hard. Then she trotted down the street to see old Mr Salter who was recovering from an operation.

Perhaps I can make him a cuppa or run an errand for him, she thought, totally unaware of the dog warden who had been spying on the meeting. He had been amazed to see the Scottie dog flying through the window

but he was more interested in the black-and-white mutt that seemed to be in charge. He looked at his crumpled photo of the snarling canine criminal and his heartbeat raced. He compared it with the dog that was crossing the road in front of him. She had the same markings, the same stupid ears. She didn't look particularly dangerous but he imagined Lara curling her top lip and was certain the reward would be his.

As Lara squeezed through Mr Salter's gate, the warden pounced. He knew she was

dangerous and that he would only get one chance. He wasn't about to waste it. He jumped out from behind a wall and caught Lara around the neck with a loop on the end of a long pole. She had no time to react. He was an expert dog catcher. She tried to run but was hauled back and pinned to the ground as the warden took his photo out once more. Now he was certain.

'OK, dangerous dog,' he hissed, 'let's see how you like this.'

Lara struggled, shaking her head, trying to get loose. *What's going on? Get this thing off me.*

The warden tightened the loop so she was nearly choking and dragged Lara to his van. Keeping her at arm's length, he forced her into the back and slammed the doors.

Lara threw herself against the side of the van. *Let me out. I think I'm being dognapped,* she howled.

The warden sprinted around to the driver's side and jumped in. Wheels spinning, the van roared down the road in search of the reward.

★

Lara couldn't work out what was going on.

It seems the whole doggie neighbourhood has been rounded up and brought to the police station, she thought as a dozen dogs were lined up in a special room.

Lara took her position as dog number twelve in the line. An old lady with a black eye entered the room, helped by a policewoman, guiding her by the elbow. The old lady doddered along the line of dogs, looking carefully at each one. She paused at number six, a Labrador, and gave him a stroke. Jimmy at number eight got a coo of delight.

'Isn't he lovely?' she smiled at the policewoman. 'And what's he done to his poor nose?'

Number nine got a very firm 'No'. Number ten got a 'Definitely not' and Sparky at number eleven got a 'Wrong colour'.

Lara sat patiently, wondering what was going on. The old lady shuffled in front of her and Lara saw the lady's mouth fall open. Her face went white and she started to shake. Lara watched in horror as the lady raised a bony finger and pointed at her.

'That's the one. That's the horrible dog that attacked me,' she cried. 'I remember the black-and-white splodges and the one ear sticking up.' The old lady burst into tears and the policewoman offered her a tissue.

Hang on a second, thought Lara. *Did you say I attacked you?*

'Are you sure, Mrs Owen?' asked the policewoman. 'Are you absolutely sure it's number twelve?'

Mrs Owen took another look and her

wailing said it all. Lara watched as she was led away, sobbing into the tissue.

This can't be right, thought Lara. *There must be some mistake. I've never attacked anyone in my life. Well, not good people anyway. Only baddies who deserved it.*

All went quiet for a moment and the dogs settled down.

'What's going on, Lara?' barked Jimmy. 'Why did that old lady point at you and burst into tears?'

'Not sure, Jimbo,' she replied. 'Something very strange is going on.'

Doggie eyes watched as the door swung open once more and a teenager entered the room. She was led in front of the line of dogs, shaking her head as she went. She didn't even get halfway before she pointed at Lara.

'That's the one,' she said, raising her finger like a cricket umpire. 'Mutt number twelve. That's the horrible dog that stole my iPod.'

Eh? Did what? thought Lara. *I've got an iPod of my own so why would I need yours? And did you call me a 'Horrible Dog'? How rude!*

The other dogs were led away.

'Keep your chin up, Lara,' yapped Jimmy. 'We know you didn't do it because you were training us all afternoon.'

Lara was alone in the room. The warden who had caught her was summoned and she was hooked round the neck once again and led away to the cells.

'Hang on,' she barked frantically, 'this isn't right. I'm innocent until proved guilty. The old lady is wrong. Whatever she says, I didn't do it.' Lara struggled and the noose tightened.

She bared her teeth and growled at the warden. 'You're strangling me, stupid. Let me go.'

Lara shook her head in desperation and the noose started to cut into her neck.

The dog catcher struggled to control the wriggling dog. 'Boy, you are a lively one,' he sneered.

He heard a series of barks and growls. He looked at the helpless dog, who now had her fangs bared, looking ready to savage him.

'Nasty dog,' he said. 'You, pooch, are sooo guilty and I am going to be sooo rich when I collect my reward.'

And you are going to be sooo sorry when you find you've made a mistake, choked Lara as she was bundled into a tiny cage in a cell. The noose was removed, the cage door slammed and Lara sucked in lungfuls of air. The dog warden disappeared to collect his reward.

Lara couldn't work out whether she was shivering from cold or fright. *What on earth is going on?* The cage was too small to pace up and down so she sat and thought about her awful day, a million things spinning around her mind. *It makes no sense.*

Night came and she tried to get some rest. Lara lay with her head on her paws and whimpered softly to herself as she fell into a restless sleep.

11. Community Service

The Cook children didn't know what to think when Lara didn't come home.

'She always meets us off the school bus,' explained Sophie to Mum. 'And I mean, always. Like all the time. There must be something really wrong for her not to be here.'

'Perhaps she's had an accident or got lost?' suggested Ben who was white with worry.

'Or dognapped by an enemy agent?' piped Ollie rather too cheerfully. 'The professor said people might try and steal her.'

Ben went whiter still. He stormed off and collected a search party of school friends to circle the neighbourhood on bikes, looking for their beloved Lara. Mum made them give up at 9 p.m. when it was getting too dark to see anyway. Ben went to bed and lay wide-eyed with worry. He would be up at dawn to start the search again. He struggled to sleep until eventually tears and tiredness overwhelmed him.

Professor Cortex hated sleeping. It got in the way of his research programme so he always kept it to a minimum. He was already in the laboratory when Ben phoned first thing the following morning. His black van broke all speed limits and pulled into the Cooks' drive exactly two hours later. A posse of black-suited agents jumped out and began scouring the area. The professor emerged and burst into the kitchen, surprising a red-eyed Mrs Cook making breakfast. The professor didn't do hellos.

'GM451,' he asked, 'is she back?'

Mum shook her head. 'No, professor,' she sniffed. 'Ben, Sophie and my husband are already out looking. We've not seen her since breakfast yesterday. No text, no phone call, no email . . . nothing.'

Ollie looked up from his cocoa pops. 'Captured by an enemy agent,' he suggested perkily.

'Quite,' smiled the professor. 'All very disturbing.' He turned to his second in command. 'I want the area searched thoroughly,' he ordered. 'Leave no stone unturned. Visit every dog shelter, barn and police station in a fifty-mile radius. I want a result by midday. Understood?'

The agent turned on his heels to organize the search. The professor poured some hot water into a mug. Without offering any to Mrs Cook, he took a jar from his pocket and poured some home-made brain-boosting powder into the water, stirring furiously.

'Think, Maximus, think.' He sipped the liquid and calmed down. 'This could be very serious indeed, Mrs Cook,' he said softly. 'If enemy agents are involved, this will have to go all the way to the Prime Minister.'

At 10.41 the professor's mobile rang. He answered it immediately.

'Yes,' he barked. Mum watched as his forehead creased into lines. 'Where? OK. Where's that? Which police station exactly?' The professor paced up and down the kitchen with a serious look on his face.

'Why? You're joking!' Mum watched the professor's face. Whoever was at the other end clearly wasn't joking. 'A bank? And a post office? An old lady . . . surely not.' He shot a worried glance at Mum. 'And she's hijacked a bus?' The professor's creases deepened. 'But she's already got an iPod. I'm on my way,' he snapped as he pocketed his mobile.

Lara had spent an uncomfortable night in the police cell. She was relieved when the door opened and in marched the professor

and the children. Ben and Sophie ran straight to the cage.

'Lara, you're alive!' cried Sophie. 'We thought you'd had an accident.'

'Or been dognapped,' added Ben, stroking his pet through the cage bars.

'Careful, lad,' said the dog warden standing nearby. 'That dog's a killer. It's a dangerous brute who's already robbed a bank and mugged an old lady.'

Ben looked the man in the eye and laughed. 'What, Lara? No chance. I mean, she does have special skills but only uses them for good. Don't you, girl?'

Lara nodded. She was enjoying the fuss, especially being tickled behind the ear. *Apparently I hijacked a bus too. Can you believe it?*

'Don't be fooled, lad,' said the warden. 'I caught the brute myself yesterday. It growled and snarled like a wolf. If I hadn't pinned it down it would have bitten me.'

Yes, well, that was because you were strangling me, thought Lara. *And I object to you making up horrible stories about me. I demand to see my lawyer.*

The police chief entered the cell and Lara listened as he listed the crimes of the canine baddie. He brought in a TV and showed a CCTV video to the professor and the children. The professor gave a low whistle.

'It certainly looks like Lara,' he agreed. 'Same markings and everything. But it can't be. Lara's trained only to do good.'

The professor spent an hour telling the police about Lara's background and all the good work she'd done. The police had to sign the Official Secrets Act before they were told of Lara's special abilities, her Spy School training and how she came to be living with the Cooks.

'So you see,' the professor finished, 'you are very lucky to have such an expert canine crime fighter on your patch. Have you never wondered why your crime figures have been so low for the last six months?'

The police chief shook his head. He still wasn't convinced. 'She's been picked out at an identity parade,' he reminded everyone. 'The old lady and the teenager were certain.'

The professor puffed out his cheeks and

scratched his head. He agreed it was puzzling.

'And I'm equally certain that someone is framing GM451. There has to be a criminal out there who is trying to get rid of her.'

Ben and Sophie looked alarmed. Lara was worried by the words 'get rid of her'. *Mmm, don't much like the sound of that.*

After a lot of talking, the professor managed to persuade the police chief to release Lara. In return Lara would help catch the real criminal dog and the mastermind behind it. The chief gave them a final warning.

'Think of it like community service. We'll be watching GM451 very, very closely,' he said. 'If she so much as drops a crisp packet or poos in the park, we'll have no choice but to rearrest her. Next time there will be no second chance. It will be jail. Or worse. Understand?'

Lara didn't like the idea of jail but 'or worse' really made her shiver.

But I don't drop litter and I most certainly do not poo in the park, thought Lara. *First thing in the morning I will get my neighbourhood-watch gang to find this evil dog and clear my name.*

12. Identity Fraud

Thursday's neighbourhood-watch meeting gave Lara the opportunity to spread the word about the dangerous dog in their neighbourhood. She was sure they would be able to track down the nasty impostor and clear her name.

'It's a proper mission,' she told the meeting. 'A chance to put your training into practice.'

The team was keen to help out and Lara watched proudly as they set about their search.

The dogs scattered to all corners of the town. The cats stayed closer to home, some preferring to curl up, saying they might go on patrol later.

Typical feline behaviour, thought Lara.

George the tortoise headed into town to

do his bit. He'd packed for a long trip.

Potter and Meg took the High Street, checking out criminals' favourite places, like the banks and the post office. They spotted a couple of drivers breaking the law but were disappointed that there was nothing out of the ordinary. Potter had just suggested they go back home (via the butcher's) when they spotted Lara across the road. They watched her trotting into the newsagent and waited a while, planning to report to her about their morning.

Two minutes later Lara trotted out of the shop with a bag in her mouth.

'Hi, Lara,' barked Meg. 'We've been searching the High Street and Market Place, keeping an eye out for that horrible dog.'

Lara nodded, unable to speak because of the bag.

Potter felt that something wasn't quite right.

'What have you bought?' he asked. 'What's in the bag, Lara?'

The black-and-white dog dropped the bag and growled, 'None of your business, ugly mutt.'

Potter was taken aback.

'Oh, right. I only asked,' he said, rather hurt that his boss should talk to him in that way.

Just then the shopkeeper ran out of the door and tried to rugby-tackle the black-and-white dog.

'Come here, mutt,' he shouted, 'and give me that bag.' He yelled to the shoppers in the square, 'This dog has stolen money from my till. Someone call the police.'

Potter and Meg raised their hackles and growled.

'So you're the impostor,' snarled Potter. 'I

suggest you give us the bag. It's two against one. And we've been trained by the world's top Spy Dog.'

Bambi snarled back, 'And you two are outnumbered by me.'

She leaped at Potter, knocking him to the ground. Meg tried to join in but was no match for Bambi's combat training. There was a ball of snarling and tangled legs and paws. The shoppers scattered. Meg and Potter were left battered and bleeding as they watched Bambi escape with the money. Potter ran after her but the black-and-white dog was too quick.

The two friends limped back home. When the real Lara saw their wounds, she called off the search. George the tortoise had made it all the way to the end of the lawn by then.

'This dog is too dangerous,' Lara barked to her team. 'Potter and Meg are to receive bravery awards, but nobody else is to go near this horrid animal. Understood?'

The dogs and cats looked at the state of Potter and Meg and shuddered. They looked at Lara and were amazed by her confidence. Lara looked at each one of them very firmly.

'The impostor is mine.'

13. Emergency Action

Lara was annoyed that Bambi had got away. But it was now Friday and Lara liked Fridays. She was about to do a bit of dusting to help Mum when the phone rang. The answer machine kicked into action and Lara cocked her head as she listened to the frantic voice on the line.

'Hello. Hello there,' it began. 'Is anybody home? This is Sheila Borrett from number eleven Melton Avenue. The house with the blue door. I need some very urgent help and didn't know who else to call.'

Lara heard Mrs Borrett tell her husband that she was talking to the answer machine. 'Well, leave a message anyway,' Lara heard him say in the background. 'It's important that someone sorts it.'

Mrs Borrett came back on, shaky and frightened. 'This may sound daft,' she said, 'but I'm ringing from my holiday in Spain. I've left my gas cooker on. Definitely on. I'm really worried that it will explode. Can someone go around right now and turn it off. It's urgent –' The phone beeped and she was cut off.

Cynthia replaced the handset and smiled at Mr Big. 'How was that?' she asked.

'Sounded convincing,' he purred. 'The next few minutes will tell.'

Yikes, thought Lara. *That's the last thing we need. Poor Mrs Borrett.*

Without a second thought, Lara tore out of the house towards Melton Avenue. She cut across the park, down Packhorse Road and past the school. Lara was racing against time. She was pleased that she'd continued her morning keep-fit routine. It was coming in handy.

Lara arrived at the blue door of number eleven, panting hard.

OK, how do I get in? she wondered. *All the windows are shut.* She sprinted around the back to check it out. *All seem locked round here too. Or are they?* she thought, noticing that the kitchen window was slightly open. She jumped up on her hind legs for a closer inspection. *It's a very small gap, but it's the only way in.*

Lara slowly started to climb up the trellis next to the window. *Here I go again*, she sighed. *A dog pretending to be a cat burglar!* She looked down at her tummy. *I wish I'd not eaten so many custard creams*, she thought. *Here goes.* She squeezed a paw through the gap, undid the catch and opened the window. Soon she was half in and half out, gasping for breath. Lara's back legs kicked as she tried to squirm in. *Come on, Lara, wriggle, girl. This is an emergency.* Minutes later she was standing in the sink and sniffing, expecting to smell gas. *Nothing. Just the normal kitchen odours. I hope I'm in the right house.* She jumped down to the floor and approached the cooker, inspecting the knobs. They were all off. Lara smacked her paw against her head. *I don't believe it. False alarm. Silly Mrs Borrett, scaring me like that. Looks like I've broken in for nothing.*

Lara trotted through the lounge, heading for the front door. She noticed a large sack by the sofa. *I wonder what that is?* She nosed in it and saw jewellery and cutlery. *Strange,* thought Lara. *What's it doing down here?* She slipped a diamond bracelet over her paw to take a closer look. *Wow, real diamonds. These must be worth a fortune. I wonder why Mrs B has left everything down here in a sack.*

Lara heard a noise and lifted her nose out of the sack. She cocked her head. *I can hear cars and slamming doors. And footsteps. I can smell people – lots of people.* She jumped out of the way as the front door splintered and a dozen armed policemen fell into the lounge.

'Paws up, mutt,' screamed the leading officer, pointing his laser handgun at Lara's forehead, the red dot feeling very uncomfortable. 'Put the jewels back. You are under arrest. Whatever you say may be used in evidence against you. Do you understand?'

Er, there must be some mistake, officer, thought Lara, raising her front paws. *This isn't what it looks like, honest. I got an emergency call. The gas was left on . . . well, actually it wasn't but I didn't know until I'd got in.*

The dog warden appeared in the doorway, armed with his noose and pole.

Oh no, not you again. Lara froze as he hoopla'd her neck once more.

The half-strangled Spy Dog was dragged outside and locked in a van with three thuggish police Alsatians.

'We've heard about you, super-dog,' they growled. 'Apparently you've turned bad. Not so super any more, eh? Caught red-handed stealing the lady's valuables. It's going to be a long jail sentence for you or . . . worse.'

Lara gulped. *Worse than a long jail sentence! I really don't like the sound of that.*

14. Visiting Hours

The next day, Lara was taken to a high-security police station in London. She spent two days alone in a tiny cage in a cell. Solitary confinement gave her plenty of time to consider what was happening.

I was set up, she told herself. *The phone call, the sack of valuables, the police tip-off. Somebody is trying to get me in serious trouble. And it looks like they've succeeded. How could I be so stupid?*

Lara was relieved when she heard she had a visitor. She could smell him way before the door opened. A policeman entered the room, accompanied by a well-dressed man with slicked-back hair.

'Your lawyer's here to see you, doggie,' said the policeman.

The lawyer looked at Lara and then at the policeman.

'Oh, right,' said the constable, realizing that the lawyer wanted to be alone with his client.

The door closed and the lawyer went over to Lara's cage. He had an unusual face, sort of expressionless. Lara was overcome by the strong smell of aftershave. He pulled up a chair and sat in front of the dog.

Weird, thought Lara. *I've never seen a face quite like it. Are you really my lawyer?* she pondered.

The man sat in silence for a while, with a painful smirk fixed on his face. Lara watched as he took a fat cigar from his pocket and lit it, puffing a cloud of smoke in her face.

Excuse me, she thought, wafting it away. *Do you mind?*

Mr Big finally broke his silence. 'We meet again,' he said calmly. 'I thought you ought to know how it feels to be on the inside of a cage.' There was silence as he drew long and hard on his cigar. 'How does it feel to lose everything?' he asked, blowing smoke rings at the dog. The man's eyes were shining.

Do I know you? thought Lara, racking her brain. *Don't think I've had the pleasure.*

'Of course, you probably don't recognize me,' con-tinued Mr Big. 'Neither my face nor my smell.'

Correct. I'd certainly remember an ugly mug like yours. Give me a clue.

'You may remember this,' said Mr Big in his posh accent. He stood up and loosened his belt. To Lara's amazement he dropped his trousers, turned away and pulled down his pants, revealing his hairy bottom.

No need for that, thought Lara, amazed that her lawyer should be dropping his trousers. She noticed some red marks on his bottom.

Her mind was racing. She looked closer. *They look like teeth marks!* Thankfully the pants were now back up and the man was tightening his belt once more.

The visitor continued through clenched teeth,

'Teeth marks, Spy Dog. *Your* teeth marks to be exact. Now do you know who I am?'

Lara shut her eyes and took a deep breath. *I don't believe it,* she thought. *Mr Big. The man who put this bullet hole in my ear. I thought you were locked up? They gave you twenty-five years.*

The man smirked. He blew some more smoke rings at Lara. 'You are supposed to be the world's top Spy Dog. The 007 of the canine world. Well, my name's Big,' he puffed. 'Mr Big. And all this time you thought I was behind bars! Now it's your turn. Isn't it hilarious?' he cackled, choking on his cigar.

So this is all your doing, thought Lara, piecing the plot together. *The evil impostor dog, the phone call about the gas alert, the sack of jewels . . .*

'Don't you just love it when a plan works out the way you want it?' sneered Mr Big, tapping his cigar ash on to the floor. 'But, of course, putting you behind bars is only the first part. The best bit happens tomorrow. And you are powerless to do anything about it.'

Mr Big opened his newspaper and held it up for Lara to see. She didn't have her glasses so she couldn't read the small print. But she could see the picture of Mr Big and the headline: 'Sir Humphrey Goldfinger to open Millennium Diamond Exhibition'.

Sir Humphrey Goldfinger. Millennium Diamond. You? No way!

'Tomorrow, dear mutt, I, Sir Humphrey Goldfinger, will pull off the biggest crime in British history while you sit here, completely helpless.' He paused for effect, taking time to blow one last grey cloud her way. 'I'll send you a postcard from Brazil.' Mr Big folded the newspaper under his arm and stood up to leave. 'Tatty bye, darling,' he waved over his shoulder. 'Enjoy your stay in this lovely hotel.'

Lara watched as Mr Big walked out of the cell. The tobacco smoke cleared, leaving Lara alone once more. *Think, Lara, think. This is going to need a Spy Dog solution.*

15. Detective Ben

Ben was distraught. Sophie was permanently red-eyed. Ollie was too young to understand so he was remaining cheerful. Dad tried to explain it to them once again.

'Look, I know it's hard to believe,' he said, 'but she was caught breaking in. She had a sack of stolen goods. She was wearing one of the lady's diamond bracelets, for heaven's sake. I mean, what other explanation can there be?'

'I don't know, but there has to be one,' shouted Ben as he stormed out of the kitchen, slamming the door behind him. 'Lara is not a criminal,' he said quietly to himself as he entered the lounge. Ben sank into the sofa, arms folded, his face like thunder. 'And I'm going to prove it.'

He took out the picture of the black-and-white snarling dog. He had to agree that it looked like Lara. He examined it closely. Why were CCTV pictures always so grainy? Ben furrowed his brow and looked closer still. He got up from the sofa and went over to the bookcase where Gran kept her magnifying glass. He peered at the photo with it.

'Exactly the same markings,' he said. 'Same nose. Same eyes.' The magnifying glass paused over the dog's ears. 'But the sticky-up ear has no bullet hole,' he gasped. He looked again, his hand shaking with excitement. He leaped from the sofa. 'How could we have missed it? Everything is perfect about this dog, except the bullet hole. That proves it can't be Lara.'

He ran to the phone, intending to ring the professor. He saw the answer-machine light blinking so he decided to check the messages first.

'Come on, come on,' he muttered as the electronic voice droned on that there was one saved message, received yesterday, at 11.36 a.m. Ben dropped the magnifying glass as he heard the anguished call from Mrs Borrett. 'The gas cooker!' he exclaimed. 'That's why Lara was in the house. She's been set up.'

Ben thought harder than he'd ever thought before. 'What would Lara want me to do?' He picked up the phone and called Professor Cortex, explaining everything he knew. Two hours later, Ben, Sophie and Ollie were in the professor's van on their way to London.

Mr Big ran through the plan one last time. 'Are we all absolutely sure what we're doing tomorrow?' he asked.

Gus nodded. 'Me and Bambi are on the roof first thing, right?'

'Right.'

'And I'm the security guard,' said Archie.

'And I'm acting normally, like all the other invited guests,' nodded Cynthia.

Mr Big beamed at the assembled team. 'And I, Sir Humphrey Goldfinger, will be opening the exhibition. Except, by the time we open, the Millennium Diamond will have gone.'

The team raised their glasses of champagne.

'To the diamond. To the best robbery in the world,' toasted the boss. 'But, most of all, to the end of Spy Dog!'

'To the end of Spy Dog,' chorused his team.

16. Paper Poisoning

Saturday morning came and Lara knew she had to escape. *The robbery will be happening today. I have to do something. But what?*

She was delighted when Ben, Sophie and Ollie burst though the door.

'Visiting time,' yelled Ben as the three children ran across the cell and stroked their pet through her cage's iron bars. 'Lara, are you OK?'

I've had better days, she thought, although she did manage to nod encouragingly. *But I'm feeling better for seeing you guys.*

Ben eyed the policeman who'd accompanied them into the room.

'Lots to tell you, Lara,' he said perkily. 'We know you're not guilty,' he whispered through the side of his mouth.

Of course I'm not guilty, thought Lara. *But can you prove it?*

Lara wagged her tail enthusiastically as the children chatted about nothing in particular. After ten minutes, the policeman signalled it was time to leave and the children reluctantly waved goodbye to their pet.

'Oh, before we go, we thought you might like this present,' said Sophie, rummaging in her bag.

She brought out a toy bone and passed it through the bars to Lara.

'Something to chew on when we've gone!' explained Ben. Lara thought she saw him wink. 'I hope it doesn't make you poorly.'

Errr, thanks, guys, she nodded. *I'll chew on it and think of you.*

Lara stuck her nose out of the bars and blew a kiss as they left. The children started down the stairs. Ben and Sophie looked very gloomy as they thought about their beloved dog, all alone. But both had hope in their hearts.

Lara was alone again. *Nice of them to bring me a prezzie,* she thought, looking at her bone. *But why did Ben say it might make me poorly? And why did he wink?* Lara sniffed the toy bone. *Nothing.* She gave it a chew. *Still nothing.* She did notice that it had a join in the middle, as if it was two halves stuck together. *I wonder?* Lara lay with the bone held tightly in her paws and tugged one end with her teeth. It moved a little and she pulled some more. *Yes!* The bone came apart and she saw a piece of paper sticking out. *Brilliant, kids. Let's see what it says.* Lara pulled the note out with her teeth and spread it on the floor.

Lara spirits rose as she ripped the note in half. *I can't eat it all in one go,* she thought, *otherwise I really will be poorly.* She chewed on it and looked at the clock on the wall. Thirty minutes to go.

★

Sir Humphrey Goldfinger loved the Natural History Museum in London, especially the huge dinosaur skeleton right by the entrance. This is where he had chosen to give his speech for the opening of the exhibition. He welcomed the distinguished ladies and gentlemen to the Millennium Diamond Exhibition. He was warm, generous and funny. The audience loved his charm.

'And in just an hour from now,' he said, 'we will open the Millennium Room and you will see the world's largest diamond. It has enough carats to keep Bugs Bunny fed for a hundred years!' he joked. Sir Humphrey waited for the polite laughter to die down. 'Ladies and gentlemen, please enjoy your tour of this fabulous museum and prepare to feast your eyes on a gem of a gem.'

There was loud applause as the master criminal swept away towards the Millennium Exhibition room. As the exhibition's main sponsor, he had easy access to it. He showed his ID badge to the short, hairy security guard.

'No need, boss,' grinned Archie as he

opened the door and let Mr Big into the high-security room.

'We have one hour,' snarled Sir Humphrey through a forced smile. 'Let the robbery begin.'

Archie stood as tall as he could and guarded the door. His eyes darted around the entrance hall and a smile lit up his face. Spy Dog was locked up, everyone was in position. Nothing could stop them now.

17. Dr Who?

Lara looked at the clock. It was 10.30: time to play poorly. *Swallowing that sheet of paper has made me feel sick so this might not be too difficult.* She lay on the floor of her cage and whimpered. She remembered her drama classes. *OK, here goes. I'm not feeling too good,* she whined. *Feel a bit icky.*

Nothing happened. Since nobody seemed to be running for help she turned up the volume. Lara squirmed a bit more and barked, as if in pain.

Ouch, my stomach. I think I've got paper poisoning, she yapped. *Somebody come and help. I'm a dying dog.*

She saw the surveillance camera zoom in on her.

Ahh, somebody has noticed, she thought. *Let's play to the audience.* Lara turned on an Oscar-winning performance. She pretended to die like she'd seen people do in the movies. She rolled over and squirmed as if her life depended on it. Who knows – perhaps it did. She held her paws to her throat and choked. *Woe is me,* she whimpered. *Dying, dying . . . hello, over here, camera . . . I said I was dying . . . and dead.* Lara twitched a bit before lying still. Within thirty seconds a policeman entered the cell and eyed her suspiciously.

'What's up, dog?' he muttered, as if he expected Lara to be able to speak.

My tum. And my head. In fact, all over, she whined, wriggling like a worm on a hook. Then, suddenly, Lara went still. She closed her eyes, slowed her breathing and waited. *Come on, man, can't you see I'm dead?*

'OK, poochie,' she heard the policeman say. 'You don't look well. I'm calling a medical team. Don't go anywhere.'

Stupid man, thought Lara, eyes half closed.

I'm locked in a cage. Where am I going to go?

The policeman jabbered on his walkie-talkie for a few seconds and then left the cell. Lara was very aware that the camera was probably still zoomed in on her, so she lay still, squinting at the door.

Come on, kids, what's the plan? Don't leave me here like this, she thought.

A moment later the door burst open and in marched a white-coated Professor Cortex and four policemen.

'Here's the dog, doctor. Apparently she's very valuable, so can you see if there's anything you can do.'

A policeman took a bunch of keys and opened the cage. Lara squinted at the professor and saw him wink as she was dragged out and pulled across the floor.

'Looks serious,' said the professor. 'We'd better take her to the surgery. Give me a hand getting her on to the stretcher.'

Lara felt lots of hands go under her limp body. She was laid on the stretcher and then she felt herself being carried away.

'What do you think it is, doc?' asked one of the policemen. He didn't want the mutt to die on his shift. 'Will she be all right?'

'Looks bad,' said the professor gravely. 'Some sort of poisoning.' He put a stethoscope to Lara's chest and pretended to listen to her heart. Next he tapped her body in several places, like he'd seen them do on *Casualty*. 'Low blood pressure,' he lied. 'She'll need an ECG in the ambulance.'

Steady, prof, thought Lara. *You're getting to enjoy this game.*

The policemen looked even more worried. They watched *Casualty* too. They didn't know what an ECG was but it sounded serious. They helped the professor carry Lara out to the waiting ambulance. 'Thank you, gentlemen,' said Professor Cortex. 'I think you may just have helped to save a life.'

He slammed the back doors of the ambulance and jumped into the driver's seat, waving as the ambulance pulled away. Professor Cortex flicked the siren on and the traffic cleared before him. 'What a great way to get through London,' he observed, as the kids leaped from their hiding place in the ambulance and crowded round Lara.

Lara was delighted to see them. She was even happier to have escaped the cramped cage. She planted a wet lick on every face she could reach and stretched her paws. Her spy mind kicked into action. There was no time to lose. She grabbed the newspaper on the dashboard and ran a paw across the word 'Museum' above the story of the Millennium Diamond Exhibition.

That's where we need to go, and quick, she urged. *We may already be too late.*

'You want to go to the Natural History Museum?' asked the professor, swerving across the traffic. 'Are you sure, GM451?'

Lara nodded. The siren blared along the streets of London and drivers panicked to get out of the way.

Put your foot down, prof, Lara pleaded. *This is a real emergency.*

18. Bomb Squad

The ambulance pulled up at the Natural History Museum. There were lots of people milling around outside. A policeman approached the professor, looking a bit surprised that three children and a dog were getting out of the ambulance.

'That was quick,' said the policeman. 'I've only this second called for help. And it's not an ambulance that I asked for, it's the bomb squad. We've had a bomb alert in the museum and we've had to evacuate everyone.'

Lara cast the professor a knowing glance. *This'll be part of the robbery,* she winked.

The professor thought quickly. 'Ahh, yes,' he said. 'I know this looks like an ambulance but we are the bomb squad.' He cleared his throat while he thought of something almost believable. *Now why would the bomb squad be driving an ambulance?* 'Ahh, yes,' he said aloud. 'All the bomb-squad vehicles got blown up last week,' he beamed, a little over-enthusiastically. 'You know, in a big bang. Kaboom!' he explained, his hands doing a volcano eruption. 'Some of these kids' dads got a bit hurt so I'm looking after them. Isn't that right, kiddies?'

Ben and Sophie tried to look sad.

Ollie hadn't a clue what was going on. 'Wow, Dad's gone kaboom,' he cooed. 'I hope he's all right?'

The professor moved on quickly. 'Let's hope this job goes better, eh, sniffer dog?'

Pardon? Sniffer dog? Oh, right. Gotcha, prof. Lara put her nose to the ground and started sniffing anything in sight. *Just act like a sniffer dog.*

She sniffed a waste bin as noisily as she could, wagging her tail hard. She sniffed a Japanese tourist. The policeman shooed her away as her wet nose went towards his trouser leg.

'OK,' he said. 'In you go.' He cleared the

crowd and unlocked the front door of the museum. 'Don't let me down,' he said as he locked Lara and the professor in. 'We don't want the Millennium Diamond to go up in smoke!'

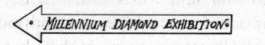

MILLENNIUM DIAMOND EXHIBITION

Lara and the professor stood in the entrance hall and marvelled at the scene. The dog let out a low whistle of amazement. *Wow. What a place!* The huge hall was dominated by the dinosaur skeleton that towered above them. There was an eerie silence, except for their footsteps echoing. Lara spotted an arrow pointing to the Millennium Diamond Exhibition and the professor followed her along a long, dark corridor. She turned into a room marked 'Creatures of the Sea' and they wandered in awe past an unimaginably huge blue whale. The professor opened one of the windows and beckoned to the children outside. They came running and quickly clambered in while the policeman wasn't looking.

'Excellent, Lara,' said Ben. 'Now we can

help you solve this crime. It's not a real
bomb, is it?'

Spot on, Ben, thought Lara. *It's more likely
to be a cover for Mr Big to steal the diamond.*

She led everyone though the corridors,
following the diamond signs. They
approached the exhibition door and Lara
signalled for everyone to shush. They tiptoed
forward and Lara pushed at the door. It
swung silently open and the crime stoppers
peered in. Professor Cortex and the children
let out a gasp of amazement.

19. Crime Time

Earlier that morning, as dawn was breaking, Gus and Bambi had taken their positions on the museum's roof.

'Nice view, Bambi,' remarked Gus. 'You can see my mum's house from up here.'

Bambi had been fixed into a harness and Gus had spent most of the morning unbolting a skylight.

After Sir Humphrey's opening speech, Archie had telephoned one of the London newspapers, telling them that a bomb had been planted in the museum.

'I hate stuffed animals, it's nasty and cruel,' he cackled down the phone. 'And I won't rest until the Natural History Museum is history.' He'd added a manic 'Ha, Ha, Ha,' for good measure, which, after he'd hung up, he considered may have been a bit overdone.

Ten minutes later the police had arrived and cleared the museum. Sir Humphrey, Archie and Cynthia had hidden in a cupboard in the Millennium Diamond room, knowing that they would be the only ones in the building.

It was 11.30 when they'd come out of hiding and seen the diamond. It had the sort of beauty that left you speechless. There it was, perched on a pedestal, just fifteen metres away. Mr Big was tempted to walk up to the diamond and snatch it, but he knew there were security laser beams everywhere. He couldn't see them but he knew they were criss-crossing the room. If anyone walked into one of those beams, the alarm would go off and they would be caught red-handed. Mr Big had done his homework. If you couldn't get the diamond from the ground, that left only one option – the roof.

Mr Big, Archie and Cynthia watched as the skylight opened and Gus's bald head poked through. Then down came Bambi in her harness, just as they'd practised. Gus took the strain and gradually lowered Bambi towards the huge diamond.

Mr Big took a camcorder from his case and captured the crime on video. He zoomed in on the dog as she hung motionless, all four legs spread, as flat as she could be. He focused on the fake diamond in her mouth. It was an exact copy of the real one. Bambi was inched down, lower and lower. It was a long drop and Gus's arms were beginning to ache.

'Steady as you go, Gus,' whispered Mr Big. 'No rush. Gently does it. Just a little further.'

Archie hopped about with excitement.

'It's going to be ours, boss. We're gonna be the richest villains in the whole wide world.'

20. A Sparkling Performance

At the door, the children held their breath as they watched Bambi being lowered towards the Millennium Diamond.

'She looks like you, Lara,' nudged Ben. 'Look at the ears.'

Lara nodded. She was trying to think of a plan, but nothing sprang to mind. *We have to do something. But what?* Her sharp eyes saw the diamond in Bambi's jaws and she sensed what was going to happen. *It's one of those now or never moments. Let's do it.*

Lara, the professor and the three children tiptoed into the Millennium Exhibition room. Bambi continued downward. The spread-eagled dog was taking orders from Cynthia.

'Flat, Bambi. Pancake. Pancake,' Cynthia said sternly.

Bambi did her best star shape, her limbs beginning to ache. Archie was doing hand signals to Gus up above.

'A bit lower,' he signalled. 'Left a bit . . . and just a tiny bit more . . . and stop.'

Bambi was dangling right above the diamond, swaying gently in her harness. Cynthia knew this next bit was crucial. She glanced at Mr Big who was puffing nervously on his cigar.

'Bambi, diamond swap,' she commanded. She hoped that all the practice would pay off. 'Diamond swap,' Cynthia repeated, calmly and sternly.

The children watched open-mouthed as Bambi's paws closed around the Millennium Diamond. She lifted it expertly before placing the fake one in its place. Bambi held the world's most expensive jewel in her paws and swung gently from side to side, waiting for her next orders.

Mr Big held his breath as he waited for the alarm to sound. There was nothing. A minute passed. The onlookers were frozen like statues while Bambi swung like a pendulum above the pedestal.

Wow, that's one clever mutt, thought Lara in grudging admiration.

Mr Big wiped the sweat from his brow and nodded to Cynthia.

'Good dog!' Cynthia reassured Bambi. 'Hold tight and back up you go.'

Archie gave the signal and Bambi started her ascent. The first pull was jerky and Bambi nearly lost the diamond, so Archie signalled to slow down.

'Gently does it, mate,' he said.

Lara had half a plan. *It's not perfect but it's the best I can do*, she thought, leaping out of

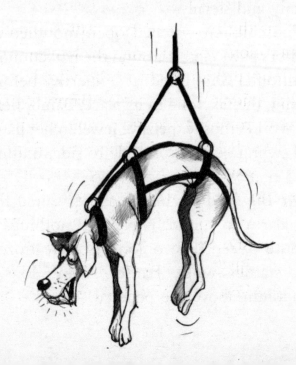

the shadows. *I can't let the gang steal the Millennium Diamond, especially as everyone will think it's me that did it.*

Lara barked wildly as she bounded into the exhibition room. Mr Big nearly dropped his cigar and Cynthia looked bewildered. Gus could see the commotion below and decided to pull harder. He tugged on the rope and jerked Bambi wildly. The diamond wobbled. He yanked the rope again and Bambi swung even more. The harness cut into her and she gasped for breath. The gem slipped from her paws and she watched in horror as it fell to the floor below.

It hit the marble with a clatter and the commotion stopped as all eyes turned on the most precious gem in the world, lying in the middle of the room. Bambi swung silently from the creaking rope, taking in the scene below. She watched the group of people standing rigid, all gazing at the diamond, nobody daring to move.

Gus's voice echoed from above. 'Sorry, boss,' he shouted.

'You will be,' growled Mr Big, chewing anxiously on the end of his cigar. 'OK, Spy

Dog,' he began calmly. 'You escaped – somehow. You are indeed a clever pooch,' he snarled, forgetting his posh accent. 'But I have you on video, stealing the Millennium Diamond,' he said, tapping his camcorder. 'This evidence will put you away forever.' Mr Big thought quickly. 'We all want that diamond, right?' he said, pointing to the gem. 'Yet we can't get it. The pedestal is surrounded by laser beams. One touch will set off the alarm and we're all caught. By the time the police arrive, my dog up there will be gone and you will be the guilty party.' Mr Big was feeling calmer. He still had the upper hand. 'And who will the police believe? A bunch of kids or Sir Humphrey Goldfinger and his video evidence?'

The retired Spy Dog was also thinking hard. *Options, Lara. Think, girl. I can trigger the alarm and get arrested? I can try to recover the camera? Or I can try to get the diamond before he does?* They all sounded too risky, especially with Ben, Sophie and Ollie around.

Mr Big was wondering how on earth he was going to get past the lasers. Riches beyond his imagination lay tantalizingly beyond his reach. He took a drag on his cigar and exhaled slowly, filling the room with smoke. As he did so, the clean white beams of the lasers came into view for a few seconds. As the smoke broke up they disappeared again. Mr Big drew another mouthful of smoke – this time a big one. He blew the smoke across the room and the lasers showed up once again. Everybody twigged at the same time and they all rushed forward a few paces before the smoke disappeared. Lara got over the first laser and Mr Big straddled another one. They were left in suspense as the criminal puffed on his cigar once more and exhaled. Lara moved quickly and silently. She fell to her belly and slid under a laser, then she stood tall and slim as she squeezed between two more beams of light. She paused motionless, waiting for the next puff of smoke. She saw that Mr Big had made good progress. He was crouched low, left leg spread out, almost as though he was playing invisible twister. In the race to the pedestal in the middle, Mr Big was clearly ahead. Another cloud of smoke came and went and Lara was now on her back, halfway under a beam of white light. The laser and smoke vanished together. *This is so frustrating,* she thought, *a bit like musical statues.* Lara was getting closer to the diamond. *Not far to go. The trouble is that Mr Big is even closer. The next move is vital.*

Archie and Cynthia watched from one side of the room, willing their mastermind towards the diamond.

'Go, boss, go,' advised Archie as another cloud of smoke revealed all the laser beams' positions.

The professor and the children watched impatiently from the other side of the room.

'Come on, Lara,' encouraged Ben. 'You can beat him to the diamond.'

Lara glanced at Mr Big. He was sweating and looked grey. *Smoking is definitely bad for you,* she thought. *What it says on the packet is correct.*

The two were neck and neck, approaching the diamond from opposite sides of the room. Mr Big was dizzy from smoking. He vowed that this would be his last-ever cigar.

One more puff will do it, thought Lara.

Mr Big breathed in . . . and all the onlookers inhaled in sympathy . . . then out . . . everyone letting their breath out together. The lasers came into view again and Lara saw her chance.

Two moves to go. She wriggled under a beam and then hopped over the next. Mr Big was on his back, sliding under his final one. Lara was there; she scuttled across the marble floor on her belly before standing in front of the priceless gem, in awe of its beauty. *Wow!* Lara held the jewel in her paws. *Yes,* she whined, *it's mine.*

'Not so quick, Spy Dog,' bellowed Mr Big, his fist coming at her. Lara ducked and he punched thin air. He was already dizzy and his wild punch caused him to sway even more. He twirled around uncontrollably and hit the floor with a thud, breaking several beams.

Bambi continued to dangle helplessly. The high-pitched security alarm rang out. It sounded painfully loud to her sensitive ears.

Lara scrambled for both jewels and was

away, the real diamond between her teeth and the fake one in her paws. She was heading for the kids.

Out, she urged. *Shoo. Scram. The security shutters are coming down in the doorways. Get out of this room quickly.*

Ben, Sophie and Ollie got out easily, but the professor was old and slow. He had no chance of escape. The security shutter was nearly down. Lara skimmed the fake diamond across the floor and through the closing shutter. Then, with the real gem held securely in her jaws, she hurled herself across the polished marble floor, sliding on her furry tummy. She lowered her sticky-up ear and closed her eyes as she shot through the narrowing gap. The shutter crunched to the floor and locked itself. The alarm was muffled.

'Nice one, Lara,' shouted Ben, taking the diamond from his pet's mouth. 'That was utterly brilliant,' he said, gaping at the spark- ling jewel that filled his hand. 'Which is the real one? This one or the one you've still got?'

Lara sniffed them both and thought hard. *I'm not too sure,* she admitted. She sniffed again. *Actually, I am sure,* she nodded, pointing to the one in Ben's hand. *The other one smells like it was manufactured in a factory and yours smells clean and natural.*

Ben passed the real diamond to Sophie who just stared in silent amazement.

Ollie eventually got his hands on it. 'Cool jewel,' he remarked, holding it up to the light. 'Mum would like it for her birthday.'

Ben pocketed one gem and Sophie the other. 'Time for calm heads. OK, so the professor's still in there but we're out and we've got the diamonds. I didn't see what happened to Mr Big and the other crooks. Do you think they're trapped?'

Not sure, shrugged Lara. *All I know is that we need to get out of here.*

Gus had done a runner, leaving Bambi to swing silently to and fro. She was disappointed that Lara had slid under the security shutter but delighted to see that Archie and Mr Big had also escaped and were following Lara. Perhaps her team would get to keep the sparkly thing after all.

The children followed Lara along the corridor. She had made them remove their shoes so they crept quietly in their socks. The only noise was Lara's paws tapping on the marble.

Which way's out? thought the dog, trotting along purposefully. She picked out a green exit sign and they turned left and then right, past the sea creatures and blue whale. *Nearly there*, thought Lara. *We'll soon be safe.*

But she was wrong. Suddenly, without warning, the group was ambushed by Mr Big. He jumped out in front of them like a bogeyman, scaring the children half to death. They ran. Ollie's socked feet took him back towards the sea creatures and blue whale. Sophie was hot on Ollie's heels and Archie was in close pursuit.

Ben darted past Mr Big and Lara went through his legs, leaving the man grasping thin air. Ben had a head start but his socks meant he was skidding around corners, unable to take them full on. It was slowing him down and he could hear Mr Big's heavy breathing close behind him. He watched Lara teetering around the next corner and tried to follow suit, but he slid on the shiny surface and came to a spinning halt on his bottom.

He looked up at Mr Big towering above him.

'Gotcha,' snarled the criminal, hauling Ben to his feet. He held the boy in a vice-like grip, with a hand across his mouth. He rummaged in Ben's pocket and found the diamond. 'Real or fake?' he bellowed, holding it up to the light.

The terrified boy just shrugged his shoulders. He genuinely couldn't remember.

Sophie and Ollie sprinted through the deserted museum, past the undersea kingdom and into the ape display. They had outrun Archie. He was some way behind, catching his breath. Sophie and her brother were glad to see so many hiding places.

'We've got the diamond so he's going to come and look for us,' panted Sophie. 'Just be calm. We can out-think him.'

The children found hiding places, Ollie

in with a stuffed gorilla and Sophie behind a Stone-Age display case. They heard footsteps and tried to control their breathing. Ollie shut his eyes and hoped. Sophie clasped the diamond, determined not to give up without a fight.

Archie entered the ape exhibition. He gazed around in awe. There was so much that reminded him of his family. He walked past a stuffed monkey with a bright-red face and stopped to stare, as if looking into a mirror. He gazed for a moment before shaking himself back to the task in hand.

'Come on, kiddies,' he coaxed. 'I know you little monkeys are in here somewhere. Uncle Archie won't hurt you . . . too much.'

Ollie gulped. Sophie took a sharp intake of breath.

Archie heard the little girl's gasp and approached the cabinet. Sophie crouched, making herself as small as she could. Archie looked at the caveman tools in the cabinet, unaware that Sophie was crouching behind it. He reached in and took a long-handled club from the display.

'This might come in handy,' he grinned, slapping the stone in the palm of his hand.

Sophie held her breath. Archie moved on and she saw him creeping towards Ollie's hiding place.

Her little brother had also been trying to hold his breath. He was snuggled behind a huge stuffed ape which, from the smell of it, hadn't been washed for centuries. He'd held back several sneezes but this one was unavoidable. '*Aatchoo!*'

Archie stopped, smiled and turned. Sophie's heart sank as she saw him heading directly towards her brother. He approached the stuffed gorilla.

'There you are, you 'orrible little brat.'

Sophie screamed as she saw Archie raise the club. Glass shattered and Ollie ran for it. Archie was after him but he tripped and fell, the club falling from his hand. As he fell he managed to catch Ollie's ankle and the little boy tumbled over. Archie grabbed Ollie's foot and held on, pulling the squirming boy back across the floor. Sophie rushed out of her hiding place, ready to offer the diamond in exchange for her brother, but she wasn't needed. She watched Ollie stretch and grab the club.

'You wouldn't, would you?' dared Archie.

Ollie's wild eyes said it all. He raised the ancient weapon and brought it crashing down on the man's arm. Archie's face went a darker shade of red and he screamed in pain as he let go of Ollie's foot. Clutching the club, Ollie ran. He and Sophie tore out into the corridor, sprinting towards the entrance hall. Archie, nursing a dead arm, lumbered after them. For some reason his injured arm was making him limp. The children burst into the entrance hall and stopped in their tracks.

In the middle of the hall, under the giant dinosaur skeleton, stood Mr Big and their elder brother. The horrible man had such a tight grip on Ben that it was making the boy's eyes water. Lara was twenty paces away from them, circling like a gunslinger. Her unblinking eyes were fixed on Mr Big. She beckoned Sophie and Ollie to her side.

We made it as far as the main entrance, she thought. *We nearly made it out. So close.*

She could see Ben's eyes wide with fear.

Don't worry, fella, she willed, *I'll find a way out of this. I promise. Not quite sure how yet, but I'll think of something.*

Lara was panicking on the inside but trying to appear calm on the outside. Sophie handed her the diamond.

Think, Lara, think. I have the gem but Mr Big has my owner. Maybe we can do a swap?

She winced as Mr Big's grip tightened and Ben's body stiffened. His eyes began to brim with tears of fear and frustration. Archie limped into the room, wild-eyed and nostrils flaring. He shook his good fist at the children and joined his boss. Mr Big showed him the diamond and he shrugged.

They don't know which is which, thought Lara.

Sophie was crying, big sobs churning from her chest.

Ollie was being brave. 'Let my brother go, you nasty man,' he ordered.

'Or what?' smirked Mr Big.

'Or . . . or I'll set my dog on you,' said Ollie defiantly. He had seen Lara do judo and was confident she could duff him up, and Archie too if need be.

'If that mutt comes anywhere near me, your brother will be very sorry,' snarled the criminal. 'Very sorry indeed. If you know what I mean.'

Ollie looked at Lara who put her paw to her lips to signify shush.

Don't worry. I know exactly what he means but it won't come to that.

Mr Big had already worked out the swap deal. He wanted the diamond not the boy and figured the dog wanted the opposite.

'OK, mutt,' he growled. 'I think we can do a deal. Your diamond for this brat.'

Archie started to hop from foot to foot. 'Yeah,' he piped up. 'We release this brat and you give us the gem. If we have both diamonds then we're bound to have the real one. Good thinking, boss.'

Lara knew she had no choice.

OK. Deal, she nodded. *My priority has to be the kids.*

She took the club from Ollie and sat the children down at the edge of the room.

Don't worry, guys. I'm sure this will turn out

all right, she hoped. *As always, I've got half a plan. I just need a little bit of luck to go with it.*

Lara dropped the diamond at her feet, where it lay glittering. Mr Big began to salivate. He could see the diamond in all its priceless glory.

'We release at the same time,' he warned. 'I let the brat go and you slide the rock to me, OK?'

Lara nodded slowly. She took up position, holding the upturned club like a hockey stick.

I will send you the diamond, hockey-style, she thought.

Lara crouched as if taking a penalty, her stick just behind the Millennium Diamond. She was sure it would slide across the floor like an ice-hockey puck.

'After three,' said Mr Big. He pulled a pistol from his jacket. 'Any funny business and you and the boy are in major trouble.'

Lara saw the gun and her heart quickened.

Now this is very serious indeed, she thought. She remembered the bullet hole in her ear, a souvenir of their previous encounter. *I have only one chance.* She remembered her hockey lessons. *I sure hope this works.*

'One,' began Mr Big.

Lara settled into hockey position, ready to send the gem across the shiny floor.

'Two,' croaked the villain, loosening his grip ever so slightly.

Lara held the club handle as tightly as she could and took aim, waiting and hoping that the next number would bring her success.

'Three,' said Mr Big, calmly and clearly, releasing Ben.

Lara put all her force behind the shot. The Millennium Diamond skimmed across the floor. She watched Mr Big's frustration because she had aimed it to his left. He dived and missed.

Ben was away, sprinting towards Lara as fast as his socks would allow him.

The Millennium Diamond crashed into the skeleton dinosaur's left foot, just as Lara had intended.

Great shot, girl, she told herself. *Now please, please, please . . .*

Mr Big sprawled on the ground as he watched the diamond smash into the dinosaur's foot. The bones cracked and the dinosaur's ankle hit the floor. The structure above him lurched to one side. The bones creaked and the dinosaur wobbled.

Archie could see what was happening and tried to raise his boss from the floor. But it was too late. Ben turned and watched the massive skeleton fall, the men disappearing under a dinosaur graveyard. When the dust settled there was no sign of the two criminals,

just a pile of prehistoric bones. Lara padded
around the hall and sniffed the diamond.

Excellent, she thought. *This is the real one.* She
picked it up in her mouth and returned to
the children, smiling through priceless teeth.

Sophie ran to her and flung her arms
around her pet. 'Lara, you are so clever and
wonderful,' she laughed. 'I knew you would
think of something.'

A job well done, agreed her pet. *We're all
safe, the men are trapped and we have recovered
the diamond. I'd say that's a good day's work.*

21. A Gem of an Idea

Lara thought hard about what to do next. She gave the diamond to Ben, who pocketed it.

We need to get to a police station, fast. I can return the diamond and then everything will be OK.

The museum's main door creaked open and in marched a small army of uniformed men.

Ahh, the real bomb squad. About time too.

The man in charge couldn't believe his eyes when he saw children in the museum and cleared them out immediately.

'This is a very dangerous mission — far too dangerous for kids to be around,' he said.

Lara wagged her tail enthusiastically. *Tell me about it!*

When he saw Lara he was even more surprised. 'Dogs are not allowed in the museum. How did you get in here, pooch? And what on earth have you lot been up to?'

Oh, you know, catching baddies, rescuing priceless diamonds . . . everyday Spy Dog stuff, smiled the family pet.

Lara and the children were ushered outside and they became lost in the crowd milling about, waiting for the museum to reopen.

Lara spotted a taxi. She stood on her hind legs and pointed. The professor was still locked in the Millennium Room so Ben took charge of hailing the cab. The taxi drew up. Lara and the three children jumped in.

'Where to?' asked the driver

Ben shrugged. 'Er, the nearest police station, I suppose,' he suggested.

Lara nodded as she sat back and relaxed.

At last, we're nearly at the end of this adventure.

The London traffic was slow. The taxi driver avoided jams by weaving through a warren of back streets.

Blimey, where are we going? thought Lara.

This must be the longest journey to a police station, ever. I'm sure we're heading the wrong way. She tapped on the glass. The driver looked round, gold teeth glinting. Sophie squealed. She recognized Gus immediately.

'I think we'll avoid the police if that's all right with you lot,' he smirked.

Lara heard the doors click as the central locking was activated.

Trapped! With a gold-toothed gorilla. She slapped her paw across her forehead. *This is so frustrating.*

'Just give me the diamond and you can go free,' sneered Gus, turning his head to speak to them. 'I promise you. I'm a man of honour.'

Yeah, right, thought Lara. She was so frustrated that she stuck her tongue out at Gus. *You are such a horrible villain.* She stuck her paws in her ears and waggled her claws at him. *I hate criminals.*

The big man had never seen a dog do that before. 'Why, you horrible, rude mutt,' he began, reaching into the back of the cab.

He took his eyes off the road for just a

moment too long and Lara saw he was going to run into the bus ahead. There was an almighty crunch and the children were thrown forward, but luckily they had their seatbelts on.

Lara quickly assessed the situation. *No harm done. Gus is pinned by the airbag. This is our chance.* She slid the window open and helped the kids out. *Quickly, everyone. No time to lose.*

She was the last out. Then they were away, haring down a side street. Lara looked back at the crumpled cab; steam was hissing out of its engine. She watched as Gus kicked the driver's door off its hinges and clambered out. His head was bleeding. He spat his gold teeth into his hand and pocketed them. Gus stood and glared at Lara, flexing his muscles like the Hulk.

Yikes! Lara turned and ran. She heard the taxi door slam and she knew the ape was after them. The children ran like never before. Lara sprinted ahead.

Come on, kids, she urged.

The lumbering ape was surprisingly fast. He drew a pistol and aimed as he ran. A bullet zinged into the pavement and the children sprinted even faster. Another bullet hit a passing car, shattering its windscreen. Lara barged through the oncoming pedestrians and people started to panic. Several passers-by pulled out mobiles and rang 999.

The big man started to slow and the children pulled ahead. Lara had a bit of breathing space.

Time to think, she panted. They were in Trafalgar Square. *Pigeons and tourists everywhere.* Lara saw a lady with a handbag and growled her most vicious growl. *Sorry, lady,* she thought, *but I need your bag.* Lara grabbed the bag in her teeth and yanked it from the woman. Lara sniffed inside. *Excellent,* she thought, pulling out a notepad and pen.

Several onlookers watched the dog hold the pen in her mouth and scribble a note. *It's the diamond he wants,* thought Lara. She took the famous gem off Ben and shooed the children away. *Go on, guys. A safe distance, please.* Lara stuck the note on a nearby red phone box. Then she sat and waited for Gus to appear. *I'm just hoping he's as stupid as he looks.*

A minute later the ape plodded into view, panting heavily, shoulders drooping with the effort of the chase. Blood was trickling down his face and people were staring. He saw Lara and a toothless snarl lit up his face. He started to push tourists out of the way, pigeons scattering as he lumbered towards the dog. She pointed to the phone box and he stopped in his tracks. He looked at the note:

Phone 07764 245635 if you want to find the real diamond

'Eh?' Gus's tiny mind whirred as he repeated the phrase in his head.

Lara watched as he fumbled in his pocket for some change and swung the heavy door open. He was halfway through the phone call when Lara wedged the door shut with the world's most famous diamond, so escape was impossible.

It makes a perfect doorstop, she thought as she admired her handiwork. *I can see why it's priceless.*

The children watched from a safe distance as the Hulk went berserk in the phone box. He punched the windows out and ripped the phone from its cradle in a terrible tantrum.

I knew I wouldn't like him when he's angry, Lara smiled.

Once again, passers-by reached for their mobiles and reported the hooligan to the police. Minutes later two police cars drew up, the diamond doorstop was removed and a handcuffed Gus taken away. Lara and the children came forward and got into the second cop car, Ben, Sophie and Ollie jabbering excitedly as they were driven safely away.

22. Stress City

Dad was secretly very proud that his children had solved a major crime. But Mum was annoyed that the children had been dragged into yet another dangerous adventure.

'You, professor, had no right to take the children to London without my permission,' she'd bellowed. 'I've been beside myself with worry. How would you feel if I'd taken your children away?' The professor hadn't got children, just dogs, but he'd still hung his head in shame. 'And you lot should have known better,' she'd yelled, turning her attention to the children. 'Sneaking off in secret. What were you thinking?'

The group knew not to answer back and tried their best to look sorry. They were thinking that Professor Cortex had been absolutely right not to ask permission. Never in a million years would Mum have allowed them to go to London and if they hadn't snuck away, they would never have got Lara back and the crime would not have been solved.

But Mum saved her loudest voice for Lara.

Yikes, cringed the family pet as Mum let rip.

'And you, madam,' she began, 'I can't believe that you let the children fall into danger. Again! Diamonds, shootings, chases across London. Spy Dog, pah! Danger Dog more like. Whatever do you think you're playing at?'

But . . . thought Lara, *but it wasn't really my fault.*

'No buts, Lara,' bellowed Mum. 'You need to learn the error of your ways, my girl. And learn you jolly well will.'

Ben and Sophie were pleased to get away with being grounded for just two weeks. Ollie was upset that his PlayStation rights were withdrawn for ten days. But everyone was relieved to have Lara back safe and to find out that the professor hadn't been blown up by the bomb squad.

Lara had the worst punishment, having to go to work with Dad for a whole month.

But I hate window cleaning, she thought. *I'm rubbish at it. I'm a highly trained secret agent, for goodness' sake. It's insulting to make me clean windows.*

Nevertheless the punishment stood.

'It's the only way that I can keep an eye on you,' said Dad. 'Be thankful it's only for a month.'

It was a while before things calmed down. Ben and Sophie were asked to tell their story yet again in the playground.

'So what happened after the bones had collapsed?' asked Jordan. 'I mean, were the men dead or anything?'

Ben shook his head. 'No, just a bit dazed. The museum manager wasn't very amused that his dinosaur had been destroyed but he understood when he heard what had happened. And, besides, the bones are already being reassembled, so there's no permanent harm done.'

'And what about the others? What about the nasty dog? The one that looks like Lara?' asked one of the children.

'Bambi is a nasty dog,' agreed Ben. 'But she's very, very clever. The professor is giving her a chance to mend her ways. She is being retrained to do good things and is doing very well. Her owners are all in prison. Mr Big won't be tunnelling out again in a hurry. We won't see him for at least twenty-five years.'

'And the other two? What about Archie and Gus? And that lady who trained the bad dog?'

'Same as Mr Big,' grinned Ben. 'All safely behind bars.'

'So another happy ending, then,' said someone from the playground crowd. 'Where's Lara? Why can't she come to school?'

Ben looked sheepish. 'She's doing a bit of punishment,' he said sadly. 'She'll be up a ladder somewhere, cleaning windows.'

Dad had arranged a special punishment for Lara. He didn't clean office blocks very often but he decided to do one now. He and Lara stood on the platform and lowered themselves down the front of the glass tower block.

This'll take forever, groaned the family pet. *I've never seen so many windows. This is so unfair.* She looked at the cars the size of toys below. *And it makes me dizzy.*

Dad did the first few windows, expertly cleaning them with his wiper blade. Lara watched.

Actually, she thought, *that looks like quite good fun. Maybe I could have a little go.*

Dad let the rope out and they dropped to the next row of windows.

'OK, girl,' he said. 'You may as well make yourself useful. Here's one with blinds down so you can have a go. Nobody'll see you. It's all yours.' Dad sat down and undid his flask of tea while Lara took the sponge in her mouth.

First the soapy water, she hummed, splashing the window. *Then we wipe it off, making sure we get in all the corners. Hey, this is OK.*

Mr Peacock was back at work after his holiday in the Lake District. His last few days there had been bliss and his nervous twitch had gone completely. He had been catching up with his emails all morning and decided it was time to open the blinds and let some sunshine in. He pulled the cord and the blind swished open, sunlight flooding into his office. He shielded his eyes from the glare.

Oh, hi! waved Lara. *I'm, er, just cleaning your windows if that's OK? Dad's having a cup of tea.* She smiled at the man, reaching into the corners with her wiper. She watched as his face twitched. *Wow, you look like you need a holiday,* she thought.

Mr Peacock pulled the cord and the blind swished shut. He furrowed his brow and sank into his chair in a daze. He rocked while he thought.

'It's the stress. Too many emails. It can't be real.' He took a deep breath and strode confidently across the room. 'Dogs don't waterski, play cricket or cook. And they most certainly do *not* clean office windows fifteen floors up,' he smiled. He paused for a minute before he swished the blind open for a second time.

Oh, hello again! shrugged Lara, busy with her cloth. *Just got this last bit to do. Soon be finished.*

The blind shut almost immediately. Mr Peacock staggered back to his desk. He pressed the button on his intercom and spoke to his secretary. 'Please ring Margaret,' he gasped, 'I have something to tell her.'

23. Priceless

The mayor looked at the gathering of locals and pets. Lara beamed. Just about everyone had turned up, including her neighbourhood-watch team. George had hitched a lift with Jimmy.

'As you all now know,' began the mayor, 'Mr and Mrs Cook's children have solved a big crime in London. They rescued the Millennium Diamond – an extremely valuable gem – and have put three crooks back behind bars.'

Warm applause filled the hall. Lara winked at Ben who was beaming with pride.

'So we thought it was worth presenting the children with a certificate of bravery, in recognition of the brilliant work they've done.'

Ollie was the first to step forward. He waved to the crowd and blew kisses, milking the moment. He shook hands with the mayor and stood while the newspaper photographer took his picture. Sophie was up next, taking the applause with a shy smile. Ben was third up, striding confidently on to the stage and shaking the mayor warmly by the hand. The three children stood onstage, grinning, hair combed and teeth shining.

Lara sat happily, watching the children receive their certificates.

Brilliant, she thought. *I only wish the mayor knew how much I helped out.*

'But, of course,' continued the silver-haired mayor, 'there was another key member of this crime-fighting gang.'

He threw a warm smile at Lara and she felt a hundred pairs of eyes boring into her. She put on her shades and raised an eyebrow, trying to look cool.

Oh, shucks, she thought. *Do I get a certificate too?*

'If Lara would like to step up on to the stage to collect her reward.'

The family pet got to her feet and jumped onstage to rapturous applause.

Thank you. Thank you, everyone, she waved until the clapping finally faded away.

The dog sat proudly, her bullet-holed ear standing to attention. The mayor opened a box and pulled out a dog collar with a massive diamond hanging from it.

Wow! Looks just like the real thing. Lara sniffed it. *Hang on,* she thought, *I think there's something you should know . . .*

The mayor fastened the collar around Lara's neck.

'The fake diamond is worthless,' he announced, 'but we thought it would remind you of this adventure and it makes an excellent decoration for a collar.'

Fake, thought Lara wide-eyed. *Er, I think you might have made a huge mistake.* She sniffed again. *In fact, I'm sure you have.*

'It's a collar for special occasions,' smiled the mayor as the crowd cheered and the flashes blinded those onstage. The noise died down, allowing the mayor to finish his speech. 'I think we all agree that, with this collar, Lara, you look a million dollars.'

Lara smiled for the cameras. The glint in her eye matched that of the Millennium Diamond around her neck.

A million dollars? she beamed. *More like priceless.*

Puffin by Post

Spy Dog Unleashed! – Andrew Cope

If you have enjoyed this book and want to read more,
then check out these other great Puffin titles.
You can order any of the following books direct with Puffin by Post:

Spy Dog • Andrew Cope • 9780141318844	£4.99
Forget 007! Meet Lara: a spy dog – the first of her kind!	

Spy Dog 2 • Andrew Cope • 9780141318851	£4.99
'We love Lara' – *Kraze Club*	

My Brother's Famous Bottom • Jeremy Strong • 9780141322384	£4.99
'Jeremy Strong is the King of Comedy' – *Guardian*	

Superloo: Hadrian's Lucky Latrine • W.C. Flushing • 9780141320052	£4.99
Join in the crazy adventures of the time-travelling toilet – one flush and it's gone!	

The Legend of Captain Crow's Teeth • Eoin Colfer • 9780141318905	£4.99
'Plenty of full-on belly laughs' – *Sunday Times*	

Just contact:

Puffin Books, C/o Bookpost, PO Box 29,
Douglas, Isle of Man, IM99 1BQ
Credit cards accepted. For further details:
Telephone: 01624 677237
Fax: 01624 670923

You can email your orders to: bookshop@enterprise.net
Or order online at: www.bookpost.co.uk

Free delivery in the UK.
Overseas customers must add £2 per book.

Prices and availability are subject to change.

Visit puffin.co.uk to find out about the latest titles, read extracts and
exclusive author interviews, and enter exciting competitions.
You can also browse thousands of Puffin books online.